DIRTY TRICKS

When Marsha got to school, she immediately realized that kids were looking at her strangely. A small crowd had gathered around a sign. When they saw Marsha they quickly went away, leaving her alone to read—"DON'T VOTE FOR A RAT."

Marsha's hand covered her open mouth. She felt her face turn a hot red.

Suddenly she saw Bobby heading down the hall. How could she face him. She couldn't face anyone. She couldn't bear to see Bobby looking at her with . . . what? Shock, disappointment, contempt? She could try to tell him the truth, but would he believe her? Bobby had told her not to campaign. He'd been right. If she'd only listened to him . . .

D0049922

Other Avon Flare Books by
Suzanne Weyn

THE MAKEOVER CLUB
THE MAKEOVER SUMMER

Avon Books are available at special quantity discounts for
bulk purchases for sales promotions, premiums, fund raising or
educational use. Special books, or book excerpts, can also be
created to fit specific needs.

For details write or telephone the office of the Director of
Special Markets, Avon Books, Dept. FP, 105 Madison Avenue,
New York, New York 10016, 212-481-5653.

THE MAKEOVER CAMPAIGN

Suzanne Weyn

AN AVON FLARE BOOK

THE MAKEOVER CAMPAIGN is an original publication of Avon Books. This work has never before appeared in book form.

AVON BOOKS
A division of
The Hearst Corporation
105 Madison Avenue
New York, New York 10016

Copyright © 1990 by Parachute Press, Inc.
Published by arrangement with Parachute Press, Inc.
Library of Congress Catalog Card Number: 89-92501
ISBN: 0-380-75850-4
RL: 4.6

All rights reserved, which includes the right to reproduce this book or portions thereof in any form whatsoever except as provided by the U.S. Copyright Law. For information address Parachute Press, Inc., 156 Fifth Avenue, Suite 325, New York, New York 10010.

First Avon Flare Printing: August 1990

AVON FLARE TRADEMARK REG. U.S. PAT. OFF. AND IN OTHER COUNTRIES, MARCA REGISTRADA, HECHO EN U.S.A.

Printed in the U.S.A.

RA   10   9   8   7   6   5   4   3   2   1

Chapter One

Rissa Lupinski made a face at the poster hanging on the wall near her locker. "I can't stand having to look at that every morning," she said to her friend Sara Marshall.

"I know," Sara agreed, shouting over the rock music blasting from the headphones of her Walkman. They stood for another half minute looking at the poster. A large black-and-white photo of Doris Gaylord smiled down at them from the center of the poster. Under her picture were written the words: DORIS GAYLORD FOR SOPHOMORE CLASS PRESIDENT. VOTE FOR THE BEST!

"The best phony, that's for sure," said Rissa. "I can't believe she can fool that many people into thinking she'd be good for our class."

"Really. And can you believe those posters? Her parents must have spent a fortune to have them printed," said Sara, pushing the earphones back over her short dyed-orange hair until they rested around her neck. "It looks like she's running for governor of the state instead of the class." Sara didn't like Doris any more than Rissa did. She'd had her share of run-ins with Doris in the past.

The hallway was becoming more crowded. Rissa turned to Sara. "The horrible part is that she'll probably win," she said above the growing din of slamming lockers. "The only one running against her is Marty Barrow."

"I know," said Sara. "I'll vote for him, but it doesn't look like he has much of a chance. I don't think too many people know who he is. He hasn't even put up one sign."

"They only took nominations yesterday. Doris must have had these signs ready to go before school even started," Rissa noted. She rolled her light blue eyes and sighed. "I can't bear the thought of hearing Doris's voice over the intercom with sophomore announcements every morning. She's a big enough egomaniac as it is. If she's class president, she'll be totally out of control. She'll never let us forget it."

Sara came closer to Rissa. "That's why I did what I did," she whispered, trying to hold back a smile. "When they announced that today was the last day for nominations, I had a great idea and I realized I had to act fast—"

"What did you do?" asked Rissa.

"I just now went down to the office and put Marsha's name on the list of candidates."

"You what?" Rissa cried in disbelief.

Sara nodded sheepishly. "I nominated Marsha to run against Doris!"

"I can't believe you did that!" Rissa shrieked.

"I think Marsha would be a great class president," said Sara. "You have to help me find a way to tell her."

"No way," said Rissa. "This was your bright idea. You tell her."

"Come on," Sara pleaded. "You know she'd be good, but she just needs a little push to—" Sara cut herself short as Marsha Kranton came around the corner.

2

"I hadn't really thought about it, but you might be right," Rissa said, running her hand thoughtfully through her short blonde hair. "She could be good in the job."

"She'd be great," said Sara.

"Who'd be great?" Marsha asked.

Sara and Rissa looked Marsha over as if seeing her for the first time. "See what I mean? She'd be perfect—really," Sara said to Rissa after a few moments.

"She is," Rissa agreed. "She even looks presidential. With a few changes, of course."

"What are you talking about?" Marsha demanded, looking puzzled.

"Of course," Sara concurred, ignoring Marsha's question. "Those contact lenses will have to go, though. She'll have to put her glasses back on. And her hair needs something, I'm not sure what. That crimped look is too floozy-ish for a president." She circled Marsha, studying her appearance with narrowed eyes. "This could really work," she said to Rissa. "And it will be very cool for us to be friends with her and all."

"But that's not why we want her to do it," said Rissa pointedly.

"Oh, no. It would be to save the Rosemont High sophomore class from having a horrible president," Sara said. "We have only noble motives here."

"Please tell me what are you talking about!" Marsha exploded.

"Okay," Rissa said. "Listen to me before you say no. We think you should run for class president."

"I bet you could win," Sara jumped in excitedly. "You're not an airhead like Doris, but you're not a super-nerd like Marty either. You're a solid middle-of-the-road candidate."

3

"Thanks," Marsha said sarcastically. "Old middle-of-the-road Marsha. How exciting." She stepped back away from Rissa and Sara. "Forget it, guys. I'm not doing it."

"Why not!" Rissa pressed.

"Why *me*? Why not one of you?"

"I'm not the presidential type," said Sara. "Look at me. Did you ever see a class president with dyed orange hair, rubber jewelry, and a torn T-shirt? I mean, come on!"

"And I'm too busy already," said Rissa. "Between basketball and modeling, I'll be lucky if I get a chance to even do my homework this year. And you know how strict my father is about grades."

Marsha sighed. "The answer is still no."

"Think about how popular it'll make you. You haven't had a guy interested in you since you and Jim broke up this summer. It's getting to be kind of a while, don't you think?" Sara insisted.

Marsha looked at the two other girls as if she were trying to decide whether or not to tell them something. "If you must know," she said hesitantly, "there is a boy who's interested in me. I kind of like him too."

Sara and Rissa's mouths dropped open in surprise. The three girls had been best friends for years, and usually told each other everything. The fact that Marsha liked someone new was a surprise to Sara and Rissa.

"Who?" Rissa asked.

A touch of pink flushed Marsha's cheeks and temples. "Bobby Turner," she blurted out.

"Marsha!" cried Rissa, clearly stunned by the news. "He's not your type."

"Why not?" Marsha challenged, miffed. "Because he's gorgeous, totally cool, and rides a motorcycle?"

4

"He's so different from the other boys you've liked," Rissa observed. "He's not smart like Jim, or even athletic like Craig Lawrence. Isn't he kind of like . . . I don't know . . . like a hoodlum type?"

"He is not a hoodlum," snapped Marsha. "You're always so conservative. You think jocks are the only boys worth dating. Bobby is sweet. I can see it in his face. He just has a dangerous air about him."

"I can understand why you'd like him," Sara commented. "He's pretty handsome. But he's a junior. How did you meet him?"

"He's repeating sophomore biology. And he sits at my lab table."

"He failed science?" said Rissa, her eyebrows raised skeptically.

"If I remember correctly, you only passed science last year by two points," said Marsha.

"Okay," Rissa grumbled. "I just don't want to see you get mixed up with someone who's not good enough for you. You've had two flopped romances in the last six months and I don't want you to go through another one."

Marsha patted Rissa on the shoulder. "Thanks, Mom," she teased, "but I can take care of myself."

"Are you sure he likes you?" asked Sara.

"Almost positive," Marsha answered. "I'm the only one he talks to in class. I just get that feeling."

"That's great, but let's get back to the subject," said Sara.

"What subject?" asked Marsha.

"The class president subject," Sara reminded her.

"I don't want to be class president," Marsha insisted.

"Come on," Sara cajoled. "You'd be great, and we'll do everything to help you beat Doris."

5

"No," Marsha insisted stubbornly. "Yesterday Bobby told me he thinks this whole class president thing is stupid. He says it's only a personality contest and the class president doesn't really do anything."

"So, that's *his* opinion," said Sara.

"Well, *his* opinion is important to *me*," said Marsha.

"Isn't my opinion important to you?" Sara challenged her.

"Sure it is," said Marsha, "but . . . this is different."

"No, it isn't, and besides, you don't have any choice."

"Why not?" asked Marsha.

"Because . . . because . . ." Sara hesitated. "Because I already signed you up, is why."

Marsha's jaw dropped. "You're joking, right?"

Sara and Rissa shook their heads in unison. "I went down to the office this morning and did it. Today is the last day for nominations," said Sara.

"I can't believe you did . . . I can't believe . . . You wouldn't," Marsha stammered.

"She could and she did," Rissa confirmed.

Marsha's eyes blazed angrily. "You had no right. None at all. You have some nerve. It's so—"

"Hold on," Rissa interrupted calmly. "You have a pretty short memory. Just last month you signed me up for the beauty contest at Hemway Park without asking me, didn't you?"

"Yeah, but I knew you could do it, and that you wouldn't enter on your own. And I was right. You were the first runner-up."

"So, it's the same thing," Rissa pointed out.

"No, it's not." Marsha sulked.

6

"How is it different?" asked Sara.

Marsha looked at the two of them, then let out a long, miserable sigh. "Because you won," she said. "I can't win this thing."

"Yes, you can. You can," said Sara. "You don't have any choice, so you might as well try."

The bell for homeroom rang. "I can't believe you did this to me," Marsha shouted as the three girls joined the flow of students in the hall and moved on toward their homerooms. "Thanks to you I have to run for class president now."

"It is not the worst thing that could happen to a person," said Rissa. "And we'll help you. I'll be your campaign manager."

"And I'll be her assistant," Sara volunteered.

"What about Bobby?" asked Marsha unhappily.

"He won't care," Sara assured her.

They turned the corner and there, standing by the doorway to Marsha's homeroom, was a tall boy with longish dark brown hair. He wore a beat-up brown bomber jacket over faded jeans. He had high cheekbones, a straight, narrow nose, and lively brown eyes.

"Hi, Bobby!" Marsha called excitedly.

Chapter Two

"Hi, Marsha," Bobby said casually, as if he always stood around outside her homeroom. "Could I talk to you a minute?"

"Sure," she said, her voice becoming just a bit high and squeaky. Rissa and Sara stood and waited beside her. "You two had better go or you'll be late for homeroom," Marsha said to them meaningfully.

"There's time," said Rissa.

"No, there isn't," Sara disagreed, pulling Rissa down the hall by the sleeve of her blue sweater.

Marsha clasped her hands together to keep them from shaking. Bobby Turner was waiting for her! This was proof! He definitely liked her.

"I missed yesterday's lab, and I was wondering if I could get your notes," he said. "I just need to find out what we did and all."

"No problem," said Marsha. "They're in my locker. It's sixteen-B. Want to meet me there after homeroom?"

"I'll meet you before lunch, okay?"

"Great," she said. "See you then."

"Thanks a lot," he said. With a casual wave he left. Marsha stood waving—her hand in the air even after he'd faded into the hallway traffic.

Bobby Turner was coming to her locker at lunchtime!

8

She nearly floated into homeroom and dreamily took her seat. She was dying to tell Rissa and Sara what Bobby had said, but she'd have to wait. In grammar school, the three girls had always sat near one another because of their last names—Kranton, Lupinski, and Marshall. And even in junior high, whenever things went in alphabetical order, they had been together. Marsha sometimes wondered if they'd become friends *because* they had always sat so close. It had been a lucky coincidence, at any rate. She'd enjoyed always having her two best friends within whispering distance.

Rosemont High had changed that. The school was so large that there were six different homerooms at each grade level. Sara and Rissa were together in the L to O room, but she was stuck in the G to K room. Not only was she separated from her friends, but G to K meant that every morning Marsha had to see Doris Gaylord and Doris's best friend Heather Irving, a thin, frizzy-haired girl who followed Doris everywhere.

Marsha looked at Doris as she tossed her soft, shiny brown hair this way and that, flirting and laughing with the two boys who sat on either side of her. One boy, Gary Herman, was throwing wadded-up pieces of loose-leaf paper at Doris, and she was laughing as if it was the cleverest, most original thing she'd ever seen anyone do. Marsha shook her head. She could never beat Doris—Miss Petite Flirty Charm herself.

Marsha folded her arms stubbornly. This whole thing was ridiculous. They could sign her up, but they couldn't force her to campaign. And if she didn't campaign, no one but Rissa and Sara would know anything about it.

As Mrs. Ritter, her homeroom teacher, began call-

9

ing the roll, the class grew quiet. Marsha drifted off into her own daydreams, doodling the name Bobby Turner over and over on the back of her spiral notebook.

"Candidate Gaylord," Mrs. Ritter called pleasantly when she reached Doris's name.

Doris sat up straight and beamed her perkiest smile at Mrs. Ritter. "Here, as usual," she chirped.

Mrs. Ritter continued down the roster. She stopped again when she got to Marsha's name. "And we have another candidate in this homeroom. I was in the office this morning, and I noticed your name on the list of nominees, Marsha."

Marsha stopped doodling and looked up sharply. All eyes in the classroom were on her. She saw Doris glaring invisible daggers her way. Marsha opened her mouth to speak, but not a sound came out.

For a moment, there was an uncomfortable silence.

"Am I mistaken, Marsha?" asked Mrs. Ritter, confused. "I was sure I saw your name."

"There's no mistake," Marsha finally spoke up. "But the only thing is, I'm not—"

"Dor-is! Dor-is!" Heather Irving shouted, cutting Marsha off. Several of Doris's friends joined in.

This is mortifying, thought Marsha, sinking slightly into her seat. But then, to her surprise, a group of kids began chanting, "Marsha! Marsha!"

"Doris! Doris!" shouted part of the class while the others continued chanting, "Marsha! Marsha!"

Mrs. Ritter clapped her hands sharply. "All right. That's enough. Keep the campaigning outside the classroom. And don't forget Marty Barrow in homeroom Two-C is also running."

The class quieted down and Mrs. Ritter continued to take attendance. Marsha realized she had been

10

pleasantly surprised by the class's response. There had been almost as many cheers for herself as there had been for Doris. She had had no idea that so many kids would support her. Okay, she had to confront the possibility that her supporters might simply be anti-Doris. But still . . . they *had* cheered for her.

She looked at Doris and saw her whispering something to Heather. Every so often they'd look at Marsha and smirk nastily. Marsha closed her eyes. She didn't want to tangle with Doris. She knew Doris played roughest when she was challenged, and there was nothing worse than being the object of Doris's anger. But soon, her mind drifted back to Bobby and stayed there until the bell rang at the end of homeroom.

As Marsha gathered her books, some of her classmates stopped at her desk to wish her good luck. Marsha smiled uncomfortably and thanked them. There was no getting out of this campaign now. It wasn't until she stood up that she realized that Doris and Heather were staring at her. Marsha pretended to be sorting through some papers. She didn't want to have to pass the two girls on the way out.

Finally they left, and she headed out the doorway—only to find them waiting in the hallway. "Thanks so much, Marsha," Doris said in a suspiciously sweet voice.

"Thanks for what?" Marsha asked cautiously.

"For entering the race, of course," Doris replied, raising her lip into a sneer. "Now the nerd vote will be split between you and Marty, and I'll be *sure* to win."

Marsha glared at her angrily. "It's true. There will be plenty of votes for Marty and me to share," she answered, imitating Doris's phony sweetness, "since

11

the airheads who would vote for you are really such a small percentage of the whole school population."

"At least I'm not just a big, boring brain, like you. I, at least, have some personality," Doris shot back.

"Personality!" Marsha sputtered. "I have—"

"Nothing to offer but good grades," Doris cut her off. "Do you honestly think the class wants to be represented by a dull, bland egghead?"

"She's got you scared, huh, Gaylord?" said Rissa, who was approaching them from the other end of the hall. Sara followed closely behind her. "I don't see you out there attacking Marty Barrow. Now you have some real competition."

"This is none of your business," said Heather.

"Sure it is," said Rissa. "I'm her campaign manager. And we are going to trample you, Doris . . ."

"And you won't even know what hit you," Sara finished for her.

"We'll see about that," Doris said angrily. She turned around and stormed down the hall. Heather hurried after her.

"What a horrible little witch!" Marsha fumed. "I want to beat her so badly. I want to get every possible vote and not have her get a single one!"

"That's the spirit!" cried Rissa. "We *are* going to beat her."

"Sure we are," said Sara, her face suddenly lighting up with enthusiasm. "I just had the greatest idea. You know the big rally the candidates always hold outside the school on election afternoon? The one where each candidate sets up his or her own campaign center?"

"Uh-huh," said Rissa.

"Well, how about if Marsha's campaign center

12

features the music of Nicky and the Eggheads!'' Sara was referring to the rock group headed by her boyfriend Nicky James. She was the lead singer and she was almost certain she could get the band to agree to help Marsha—especially since they hadn't had a gig in weeks.

"That would be wonderful!" said Rissa. "See! With us on your side you can't lose. Come on," she said, heading down the hall. "We're going to be late for our first-period classes."

"I have a history test next and I'm totally unprepared," said Sara despairingly as they walked. "Yesterday's band practice seemed to take forever. Nicky kept messing up his part. And that's not like him."

"Everyone's entitled to an off day," said Rissa. "Speaking of off days, I wish I was off from school today. We're having a quiz on *The Great Gatsby* in English this period, and I've only read half of it. Didn't you read it last year in honors English, Marsha?"

"Uh, what?" asked Marsha.

"*The Great Gatsby*. I need to know what happens."

"Ummm . . . he dies," said Marsha, still sounding distracted.

"Who dies?" cried Rissa, frustrated by Marsha's vagueness. "Which character?"

But Marsha didn't seem to hear her. "See you guys later," she muttered as she turned the hallway corner and headed for her honors math class.

Marsha hardly heard anything her teachers said all morning. She was too busy trying to visualize herself as class president. She conjured the image of herself smiling and waving to her classmates in the auditorium. She pictured herself behind the microphone delivering her acceptance speech. Everyone in the school would know her then.

She would have achieved popularity. That—she had to admit—was important to her. *Very* important.

Marsha had become more confident after she, Rissa, and Sara had undertaken their makeovers. As freshmen they'd formed the Makeover Club to change themselves from little girls to glamorous high schoolers. And although Marsha hardly considered herself glamorous she had to admit that the Makeover Club had made a big change in them all.

Rissa's change had been the most remarkable. She'd gone from being a sturdy, slightly stocky jock to a graceful beauty. In fact, her makeover had been so successful that she even won a contest and landed a modeling contract.

Sara, too, had found a look that was uniquely her own. Her spiky red hair, colorful clothing, and off-beat makeup might not be for everyone, but it seemed to suit Sara perfectly.

Marsha's improvement was more subtle. She'd lost weight, replaced her glasses with contacts, changed her hairstyle, and become more daring with her clothing. But she was still shy. And shy people didn't usually become popular.

If she were elected class president, she'd be at the center of everything that was happening at Rosemont. She'd be on the inside, not the outside.

As the morning progressed, the idea of running began to seem better and better. Yes, she did want to be class president. But, every time she pictured herself winning, a second picture would enter her mind. This picture was of Doris standing behind the microphone, gloating over her victory, and staring down at Marsha, who was slumped in a chair in the first row. This Marsha was depressed and embarrassed after receiving no more than three votes—one from Sara, one from Rissa, and her own. It was complete humiliation.

Marsha became so absorbed in these thoughts that she almost forgot about meeting Bobby at lunchtime. But when the bell finally rang, his image popped into her mind.

There was something about Bobby that made her heart race whenever he spoke to her. He looked tough, but he didn't seem it when they talked. He was quiet, but he had a nice smile.

And then there were his eyes.

There was something in his brown eyes that thrilled her. He seemed to really absorb everything around him. When he looked at her it was as if he were seeing something in her that no one else could see— something that he liked.

When Marsha got to her locker, Bobby was already there. He greeted her with a smile. "Hi," she said, trying to sound relaxed. Marsha stared down at the combination to her locker. Her mind was blank. She couldn't believe it. She was so nervous that she couldn't recall a single number of her combination! She looked up at him helplessly. "You're not going to believe this, but I can't remember my combination."

"Ha! And here I thought you were such a brain!" he teased.

"I'm not such a brain, but I can usually remember my combination." She laughed nervously. "Give me a minute. . . . Five, seven . . . no . . . five, eight . . . no, that's my gym locker."

"It's not important," said Bobby, pushing his dark hair away from his eyes.

"No, no, I can remember it. Wait . . ." said Marsha, mortified.

15

"Forget it." Bobby laughed. "I probably remember the lab stuff from last year, anyway."

"I don't know what's the matter with me," Marsha said, apologetically.

"Look, it's not important," he said, leaning against her locker. "Really, it was just an excuse to talk to you. I was wondering if you'd like to go to a movie with me tomorrow night."

Marsha blinked. Had she heard him right?

Yes, she'd heard him correctly. This was too wonderful. Too wonderful to be true. She felt almost certain he could hear her heart slamming against her chest. *Yes! Yes!* she wanted to shout. She even felt faint for a split second. She had been right all along. He did like her.

"Sure, why not," she said.

"Great! I'll come get you at six?"

"I have to tell you where I live."

"No problem," he said, smiling shyly. "I looked it up in the phone book already."

"Oh," Marsha said, smiling brightly at him.

"See you at six," he said, heading down the hallway.

When he was out of sight, she turned and leaned against the locker, smiling so hard it hurt her cheeks. *All right!* she thought. In less than twenty-four hours she would be going out with Bobby Turner!

Chapter Three

"You're sure to win," Sara said to Marsha.

"No question about it," added Rissa, who sat cross-legged on the floor of Sara's bedroom printing MARSHA KRANTON FOR PRESIDENT in bold letters on a piece of oaktag. It was Friday afternoon and the three girls had met after school to map out Marsha's campaign.

"You know," Marsha said, "I'm starting to think it just might be possible." Everything seemed possible now that Bobby had asked her out.

"Okay!" Rissa cheered. She settled down on a straight-back chair, her long legs stretched out in front of her. "We have to work on your image," she told Marsha.

"I like my image the way it is," Marsha protested. "I mean, I've worked hard enough on it, don't you think?"

"We all have," Sara concurred, remembering the Makeover Club.

"Well, we have to work on another makeover for you," Rissa stated. "The old Marsha from the premakeover days was more of a presidential type. The first thing you have to do is pop out those lenses and put your glasses back on."

"No way," said Marsha firmly.

Rissa ignored her. "Second, I think you should start wearing your hair in a bun."

"Absolutely, positively no way!" Marsha shouted.

"All right. Tie it back with a ribbon, then," Rissa conceded. "But you can't keep crimping it. I don't like the way it looks that way, anyway."

"I do," Sara disagreed.

"What would a person with orange hair know?" stated Rissa, who could never quite figure out Sara's taste in anything.

"I know originality when I see it," Sara defended herself. She'd grown used to Rissa's criticism of her wild clothing, makeup, and hair. It didn't bother her anymore. Rissa was a jock and Sara was a rocker. Just because they were friends, they didn't have to be clones.

Rissa turned her attention back to Marsha. "No jeans to school. Wear a skirt every single day. It creates a businesslike look. And for starters, tuck your shirt in."

"Where are you getting this information from?" asked Sara, beginning to feel sorry for Marsha, who was tucking her shirt into her jeans.

"Remember when I was modeling in that ad for learning aides? That's how they made me dress. The ad said: 'The Serious Student Wants Serious Tools,' " Rissa told her.

"I never saw that one," said Marsha.

"It's in a teacher's magazine," Rissa told her. "It hasn't been printed yet. The point is, that's the image of the serious student. That's what you want to look like."

"Why?" asked Marsha.

"Because, look at it. Doris is going to win with her crowd, but the rest of the school might see her as

18

a snotty airhead. And I'm sorry, but Marty is too much of a nerd to represent the class. It wouldn't look good. You, Marsha Kranton, provide a sensible choice."

"It's true," Sara agreed. "If you're too much like Doris, then she might beat you. Face it, nobody can out-cute Doris. You should be clearly different."

"I don't know," said Marsha, wondering what Bobby would think of her if she changed her looks. After all, didn't he like her the way she was?

"Do you want Doris to beat you?" Rissa challenged her.

"No," Marsha admitted.

"Then leave it to me. I know what I'm talking about."

At that moment, the sound of someone singing in a full soprano came from outside the room. "La, la, la, la, la, la, la, la, la," the voice sang up and down the scale.

"Elaine," Sara explained, rolling her eyes. Elaine was Sara's older sister. She studied opera in the city. Sara loathed opera and had enjoyed the peace of having Elaine studying in Europe for the summer. But now her sister was back, and every evening the house was filled with the sound of her practicing.

Elaine continued singing her scales. "How can you stand that?" asked Rissa, covering her ears.

"I can't," said Sara, picking up her Walkman from the dresser. "That's why I always have these earphones on."

"I like opera," offered Marsha timidly.

"Figures," laughed Rissa. "Opera is something a super-brain would like."

"So I'm smart. Is that a crime?" Marsha snapped.

"Did I say there was anything wrong with it?" Rissa shot back. "I just stated a fact."

Marsha couldn't stay annoyed. She was too excited about her date. She'd told Rissa and Sara about it right after school. Now she wished she had more people to tell. She wanted to tell the whole world that she was going out with Bobby Turner!

"What are you grinning about?" asked Rissa, noticing Marsha's expression.

"I just keep thinking about my date with Bobby," Marsha answered.

"I don't know," Rissa mused. "I still don't think Bobby is right for you. Plus, he doesn't present a very good presidential image. And you're going to be concentrating on him instead of what's important."

"You have a boyfriend and you still do other things," Marsha pointed out.

"I'm not you. You go all gaga whenever a boy comes in on the scene."

"That's not fair," Marsha argued.

Sara glanced quickly at the digital clock on her dresser. It was four-thirty. "Shoot! We're going to be late to practice. Come on."

Sara had decided it would be a good thing if Marsha came to band practice with her so that she could get to know the guys in Nicky and the Eggheads better. That way they could discuss plans for the big campaign rally.

The three of them hurried down the stairs, and headed outside, down the block and down two more streets until they reached the blue shingled house where Stingo, the band's drummer, lived.

They went around to the side and Sara knocked on the door. A tall boy with long blond hair and a

20

half-moon earring in one ear answered. "Hi, Nicky," said Sara, her face breaking into a bright smile at the sight of her boyfriend.

"Hello," he replied with his throaty English accent. He kissed her lightly on the lips before he noticed Marsha and Rissa. "Hi there. You sitting in on practice tonight?" he asked.

Marsha nodded. "Your hair is getting really long," she commented.

"Yeah." He smiled self-consciously. "I've already had a mohawk and a crew cut. I decided to try long hair this time. It's really a pain, though. Takes too long to dry after washing it."

"I think it looks great," said Sara. "Very sexy. Everything looks cute on you."

Nicky blushed shyly. "Sara!"

"It's true. I can't help it if I think you're great," said Sara, taking his hand. She was eager to make him happy. Lately he'd seemed a little down, as if he had some problem weighing on his mind. Sara had asked him what was wrong, but he'd said nothing was the matter. Sara knew that wasn't true.

"I liked your hair better short," said Rissa honestly.

"Don't listen to her," said Sara. "She's totally conservative." Sometimes she wished Rissa would be less blunt—especially when Sara was trying to lift Nicky's spirits.

Nicky shrugged good-naturedly. "Everyone to their own taste."

Sara waved for Marsha and Rissa to enter. "I have something important to ask you and the guys," she said to Nicky. "Let's talk about it downstairs, though."

They went downstairs to Stingo's finished basement. The other band members were already there. They sat on the couch across from the microphones

21

and amplifiers the band had bought with money they had earned from their previous jobs. "Hi," said a stocky boy whose dark hair was cut short at the sides and grew long down his back.

"Hi, Stingo, guys," said Sara, waving at all of them. "You know Marsha and Rissa, right?"

Stingo and two other boys—Sam the lead guitarist and Eric the keyboard player—greeted the girls. Then they took their places behind the microphones.

Nicky picked up his saxophone but he didn't join them. Instead, he stood next to Sara and said, "We have to change this no-job streak we've been on, guys. We haven't had a gig since we played at Hemway Park last month."

"How can we get out of this slump?" asked Stingo, sitting down behind his drums.

"I don't know," said Nicky. "Maybe we should write new songs."

"Maybe we're going to have to do a few gigs for free, just to remind people that we're here—and available for jobs," said Sam, tuning his guitar.

"That's not a bad idea," Nicky agreed. "But where—"

Sara saw her chance to jump in. "I know the perfect place," she said. "Marsha is running for class president. There's a big rally for all the candidates on election day. If we played at Marsha's rally, we'd be performing in front of the whole school." Sara knew she was being a touch dishonest by making it seem as if she had just thought of the idea that second, but she didn't see any harm in it. The timing had been too perfect.

"That's not a bad idea," said Sam.

"Now wait a minute," said Nicky. "How do we know we agree with your policies?"

"What policies?" asked Marsha.

"You must be running on some issues. Aren't you?" said Nicky.

"I hadn't thought of any," Marsha admitted.

"Nicky, you know who she's running against, don't you? Doris Gaylord," Rissa spoke up. "You must have seen her signs all over the school."

"I hadn't really paid much attention," said Nicky. "But that's a good enough issue for me." He laughed. "I couldn't bear to see that snot at every assembly. Count me in."

Sara jumped up and down and then threw her arms around Nicky. "The whole school will be there. We'll get lots of jobs out of it—you'll see," she squealed happily.

"Thanks," Marsha said.

"We'll even write a special song for you," said Sara.

"About me?" asked Marsha, looking pleasantly embarrassed.

Just then, the side door slammed and Stingo's brother Stu came down the stairs.

And behind him was Bobby Turner.

Chapter Four

Marsha quickly ducked back into the small basement bathroom and shut the door behind her. She turned on the light, pulled some pale pink lipstick from her bag, and quickly put it on. Then she ran her fingers through her hair trying to give it a wind-tossed look, but it flopped back limply to the sides.

Pulling open the medicine cabinet she quickly grabbed a can of hair mousse. The minute she squirted it on her hair, she realized her mistake. It was shaving cream! *Calm down, Marsha,* she scolded herself. *You're panicking and not thinking straight.* The front right pieces of her hair now hung limply in a clump. She tried to bend it into a curl, but it wouldn't cooperate. Giving up, she stuck the damp hair behind her ears.

Marsha pulled out her man-tailored shirt which had been tucked neatly into her jeans. She checked her look in the small mirror and opened the second button on her shirt. She undid the third one and then lost her nerve. As she started to rebutton it, the small white button below it popped off. "Darn!" she grumbled under her breath.

Her shirt gaped open. She couldn't go out like that. Hoping to find a safety pin, she poked around on the lower shelf of the two-level shelving unit on the wall. No safety pins there. The shelf above it was a little too high for her to reach, but small, colorful boxes sat on top of it. Maybe there were pins in one of them. Standing on her toes, she reached up and tried to pull down a box.

CRASH!

The entire unit smashed to the floor, scattering its contents everywhere.

A second later there was a knock at the door. "You okay in there?" called Rissa. "Marsha? Are you okay?"

Marsha leaned against the door. "I'm fine," she whispered, embarrassed.

"Open up, I can't hear you," said Rissa in a loud voice.

Marsha turned the knob to open the door. It wouldn't budge. She jiggled it again. Still, it remained shut. "Oh, no," Marsha moaned to herself.

"What's the matter?" Rissa asked, in a voice that sounded horrifyingly loud to Marsha.

"The door is stuck," Marsha whispered.

Rissa turned the knob from the other side. "You're right." Several thuds told Marsha that Rissa was pushing against the door. It wouldn't budge.

"You're sure you didn't lock it?" she asked.

"Yes, I'm sure," Marsha replied irritably. "And don't talk so—"

"Hey, Stingo, your door is stuck," Marsha heard Rissa shout. Marsha shut her eyes miserably. *I can always count on Rissa to be quiet and discreet,* she thought.

Immediately the door was pounded, thumped, and banged on as the boys tried to open it. Someone slid a plastic bank card in through the crack in the door in an unsuccessful effort to spring the lock.

"Here, this always works," she heard Stingo say. Then came a series of drumlike raps around the doorknob. "And . . ." Stingo said triumphantly, yanking on the doorknob.

"And nothing," she could hear Nicky finish.

"Hang on, Marsha. We'll get you out," Sara said encouragingly.

"Is that Marsha Kranton in there?" she heard Bobby ask.

"The one and only." Nicky laughed.

Marsha sat cross-legged on the floor and buried her face in her hands. *Is that Marsha Kranton in there?* Bobby's words echoed in her head. *Yes, it is I, Marsha Kranton,* she thought with a forlorn smile. *Marsha Kranton, always cool, collected, and in control. Marsha the Menace. Klutz Kranton. I'm sure this is really impressing Bobby.* It seemed to Marsha that this was the story of her life. She was forever tripping, getting stuck, ripping her clothing. She hoped that someday she'd develop grace and poise, because she certainly didn't have any now.

She half hoped they would never get the door open. At this point she was so mortified she wanted to stay in the bathroom forever. She began gathering up the broken shelving unit and its contents while, on the other side, her friends continued to fool with the door. Strewn on the floor were nails, pennies, toenail clippers, pill bottles . . . but no pins.

Suddenly the door was lifted completely out of the doorway. Where it had been stood Bobby, with a screwdriver in his hand. Marsha rose, holding pieces of the broken shelving in one hand, and clutching her gaping shirt with the other. "You took the door off the hinges?" she gasped.

"You wanted to get out, didn't you," he replied.

The others stood behind him, looking into the bathroom. Marsha noticed Stingo staring at the broken shelf. "Sorry," she said awkwardly. "The shelf kind of fell down."

"It's okay," he said. "My father finished this basement himself. He's not exactly a master carpenter, as you may have noticed. Stuff is always collapsing or getting stuck."

"Well, I'm very sorry, anyway," Marsha repeated.

"No problem," said Stingo's brother Stu. "Good thing my man Bobby was here. He sure knows his stuff." He patted Bobby on the back.

Bobby brushed off the compliment. "My dad is always making me do stuff with him around the house, that's all." He met Marsha's eyes. "You look a little pale. You okay?"

"Yeah, I guess so," she said, putting the shelving down on the floor. Bobby and the other boys went back over to the band area. "Give me your sweater," Marsha told Rissa, who stood just outside the door.

"How come?" she asked.

"Just give it to me," Marsha hissed. "I popped a button."

"Okay, cool out," said Rissa, pulling the sweater over her head. Marsha put it on and pulled up the sleeves. It was much too big for her, but it was better than having her shirt gaping open.

Rissa and Sara stepped into the bathroom. "You certainly demolished this place," Rissa commented.

"It wasn't her fault," said Sara. They turned to go back out. "Aren't you coming?" Sara asked Marsha.

"Why, so Bobby can cancel our date? He's probably afraid to go out with me now."

"Don't be dumb," said Sara, pulling Marsha along by her arm.

Stepping back outside Marsha saw Bobby admiring Sam's guitar. A black motorcycle helmet sat on the sofa behind him. "Do you play with these guys?" he asked her.

Marsha was flattered that he thought she might be a member of a rock group. It even cheered her up a little. She wished she could say yes.

"Marsha isn't a rocker," said Nicky. "She is a presidential candidate."

Bobby seemed confused. "What?"

"I'm running for class president," Marsha explained edgily. She wasn't sure how he would respond to the news. She knew he didn't think much of the elections.

"How come you didn't mention it?" he asked, wearing an expression that revealed nothing.

Marsha shrugged. "I had other things on my mind, I guess."

Bobby looked at Marsha as though he were seeing her in a new light.

"I probably won't win, but you never know," she said, unable to look him in the eye. "Can't tell unless you try. Besides, you know, what do I have to lose? It will be a life experience, I guess," Marsha rambled nervously.

"Do you need that kind of life experience?" he asked.

"Experience is experience," Marsha said.

"I suppose, but . . . it seems like a waste of time to me."

"Well, I—"

"Hey, Bobby," Stu called from the stairs. "Let's get going. I want to get some riding time in before it gets too dark."

"Stu just got a new motorcycle," Bobby said to Marsha. "Got to go. See you tomorrow?"

"Tomorrow," Marsha said, relieved he hadn't backed out of their date. She'd thought he might—now that he knew she was a presidential candidate as well as someone who jammed doors and knocked down shelves.

"That Bobby is too cool," said Stingo, after Bobby had left. Stingo played a quick riff on the rim of his drums. "He just got the street bike, but you should see him on a dirt bike. That guy wins every race. He really flies!"

"He's a mean guitarist, too," said Sam.

Marsha looked over at Rissa. She raised her eyebrows as if to say, *See? They know he's the greatest, too.* She knew Rissa didn't understand how sensible, down-to-earth Marsha could be crazy about someone like Bobby. She didn't entirely understand herself. She had always pictured herself with a more sensible-looking boy. But she'd broken off with nice, ordinary Jim because it had all been too unexciting.

Marsha knew that deep down inside, she wasn't as sensible as she might seem to others. She longed to break out of her shell. Changing her looks last year just hadn't been enough. She had to find a way to bring the new person she was inside to the outside. If only she weren't so shy.

Marsha found it all a little frightening. Maybe she was some kind of wild woman trapped in the body of a sensible person. Maybe someday someone would do a special talk show about girls like her. She could see herself on the panel. She'd be dressed in black leather, wearing dark sunglasses. She'd say, "Yes, I know you'll find this impossible to believe, but I once ran for class president."

29

Rissa joined her on the couch. The two of them sat and listened as the band ran through two of their original songs. First they played "Warrior," which had a hard beat. Sara sang it passionately in her husky alto. "The Beauty Inside Out" was next. Sara had written this song herself. It was all about the three girls' efforts to make themselves over and about their friendship. It was always a big crowd-pleaser whenever the Eggheads performed it.

"Sara keeps getting better and better," Marsha whispered to Rissa.

Rissa nodded. "Having them play for your campaign is going to be great."

Marsha admired the way Sara had thrown herself into working with the band. She envied the fact that Sara had her music and Rissa had her modeling career. What did she have? Debate? She had to admit that the thrill of debate team had worn off. And, besides, if she did join again this year, she'd be partnered with her old boyfriend, Jim. Now they were just friends, but the relationship was still awkward. She wanted to try something new—to meet new people. Maybe being class president would be just what she was searching for. If only Bobby understood.

"Bobby didn't seem thrilled that I was running," Marsha whispered to Rissa.

"He'll get used to it," Rissa whispered back. "Listen, I have to watch the little monsters tonight," she said, referring to her younger brothers. "Want to sleep over? I'll invite Sara too."

"I'll ask," said Marsha. The band finished the song, and Rissa and Marsha applauded. As the band began working on a rendition of "Rock Around the

Clock,'' Marsha and Rissa noticed it was getting late and decided to leave.

Before they left, they told Sara about the sleep-over plan. She said she'd ask her parents. Marsha and Rissa said good-bye to the others and headed toward home. They walked together until Rissa turned down Fordham Street to her house. "Come over around seven," she called to Marsha.

"Okay," said Marsha, continuing up Hillside Avenue. It took her another ten minutes to get home. She walked across the front lawn as her mother was pulling her old brown hatchback into the driveway.

"Hi there. How was school?" Marsha's mother greeted her as she slid out the front seat, balancing a grocery bag in one arm and her heavy briefcase in the other. She kicked the door shut behind her.

"Okay," Marsha replied, taking the bag from her mother. "How was school for you?" Marsha's mother taught English at the local community college.

"It's hard to go back after taking the summer off," Mrs. Kranton admitted, running a hand through her short salt-and-pepper-colored hair.

They walked together into the house. Marsha told her mother about running for class president. "I think that's marvelous," said her mother, turning the key in the lock. "You'd make a wonderful president."

"That's what Rissa and Sara say, but I'm not so sure," Marsha told her.

"Just remember to tuck in your shirt and you'll be fine," her mother added, taking in Marsha's appearance.

"Mom!" Marsha groaned. Her mother could be so uncool at times! She followed her mother into the kitchen and together they began putting away the

31

groceries. "Can I sleep at Rissa's tonight?" Marsha asked. "We want to work on my campaign."

"Sure," said her mother. "I guess you've had a pretty exciting day today."

"Something else happened today too," Marsha said casually.

"What?" asked her mother, putting the meat into the freezer.

"A boy asked me to go to the movies tomorrow night," Marsha said as she stacked cans in the pantry. She didn't want her mother to think it was any big deal. Up until now she'd gone on group dates, or—when she'd gone out with Jim—they'd done things together during the day. She'd never been on a real, nighttime, one-boy out-alone date before.

"Who is this boy?" asked her mother, putting away groceries as she spoke.

Marsha took that as a good sign. "Bobby Turner."

"Ruth Turner's son?" Mrs. Kranton asked. She stopped midway to the freezer, still holding a pound of beef in her hand.

Marsha shrugged. It was hard to think of Bobby as being anyone's son. He seemed too cool to have parents.

"Doesn't he ride a motorcycle?" her mother asked.

"He might," Marsha replied evasively.

"Isn't he a senior?" she asked, skeptically.

"Junior," Marsha quickly corrected her.

Mrs. Kranton sat at the kitchen table. "I don't know, Marsha. I don't think he's the kind of boy I'd want you to date."

"What do you mean? You don't even know him!" Marsha cried.

Mrs. Kranton shot Marsha a warning look. "You're not dating anyone unless I give you my permission.

32

And I can tell you right now, you are forbidden to ride on that motorcycle.''

''But, Mom! Why?''

''It is much too dangerous.''

''But I *can* go on the date?''

''I'll talk to your father about it,'' Mrs. Kranton said, returning to the grocery bags.

''I don't believe this!'' Marsha shouted, throwing a pack of paper napkins down on the counter.

''Watch it, young lady,'' warned Mrs. Kranton, ''or you're not going anywhere.''

Chapter Five

"You look great, Dad," Rissa gently teased her father as he adjusted his tie in the hall mirror. He grunted at her, preoccupied with his task. Rissa rarely saw her tall, stocky father this dressed up. He worked as a mechanic for the airlines and came home every night in the casual clothes he wore under his coveralls. But tonight he was obviously taking his girlfriend out somewhere special.

"Is it Mary's birthday?" Rissa asked.

"No, no," her father answered absently. "I just thought I'd take her out for a nice dinner." He turned from the mirror toward his daughter. "How do I look, Clarissa?"

"Dad! You didn't even hear me before. I said you looked good. And please try not to call me Clarissa. I hate that name."

"Clarissa Jean is a perfectly fine name. Your mother was Jean Clarissa." Rissa's mother had died when she was only six, leaving her father to raise Rissa and her four brothers.

Mr. Lupinski moved into the living room and sat on the couch.

"Do you feel okay?" Rissa asked.

"I'm all right," he said. "Just had a long day."

Pete Lupinski was a quiet, sturdy man. Rissa

couldn't ever remember a time when he'd been this shaken. After a moment, he seemed to regain his old ruddy-faced composure. "Make sure Harry and Ralph are in bed by nine. No more letting them stay up for an extra program like the last time."

"Okay. I promise. But it was Friday and I didn't see the harm—"

"Nine o'clock," he cut in firmly. "And your friends can stay over, but I want you to be aware of the twins and Fred."

Rissa felt the old frustration creeping back into her. Whatever was bothering her father wasn't stopping him from being his usual strict self. It was as if he assumed all his children were forever plotting to get into trouble at any second. She wanted to say to him, *All right, already! Hurry up and leave!* But she just nodded her head.

Mr. Lupinski walked out the door, giving her unnecessary instructions to the very end. She shut the door behind him and sighed. The house was quiet for a change—but not for long. Two minutes later, Rissa heard a cry coming from the den.

Rissa hurried through the kitchen to the back of the house and found her nine-year-old twin brothers hitting each other with black videocassette boxes. "I want to watch *E.T.*" Harry shouted.

"He's seen *E.T.* a zillion times. I never get to see *Ghostbusters*!" Ralph yelled back, giving Harry another whack on his arm with the box.

Rissa grabbed the video boxes away from them. "Are you guys going to fight about this every single night?" She reached into the shelf under the VCR, pulled out a tape, and stuck it into the player. "Here, watch *Jaws* and be quiet."

"No fair!" cried Ralph, stomping out of the room.

Rissa was about to call him back when the doorbell rang. Thinking it was Sara and Marsha, Rissa ran to get the door. She was wrong. Instead, a good-looking boy with vivid blue eyes and curly brown hair stood outside.

"Mike!" she cried, happy to see her boyfriend. Then her face grew serious. "What are you doing here?"

"Nice greeting." He laughed, stepping inside. He stooped and picked up a letter that had fallen under the front hall table where the family always tossed the mail.

"We weren't supposed to do something tonight, where we?" asked Rissa.

"No," he said, handing Rissa the letter. "I came by to take a look at Roger's car. He says it's stalling out on him. I've been promising to check it out for a while. Where is that weirdo brother of yours, anyway?"

"Working at Burger Heaven," she said. "He took the bus, though. The car's in the garage if you want to look at it." Turning the letter over in her hand, she was surprised to see that it was addressed to her. "Oh, Mike," she whispered excitedly. "This is from *Teen Today*."

Teen Today was the magazine which had sponsored the makeover contest. Last March, Rissa had been one of the finalists to win a one-year modeling contract. She, like the other finalists, still had a chance of winning first place. The first-place winner was to become the national spokesperson for the magazine. With trembling hands she tore open the envelope.

It took only a second to see that the letter contained bad news. *Dear Ms. Sky,* it began, addressing

36

Rissa by her modeling name of Rissa Sky. *We regret to inform you . . .*

Rissa threw herself dejectedly into the armchair near the door. "Ow!" she cried, pulling one of her brother Fred's weights out from under her. Suddenly she burst into tears.

"Did you hurt yourself?" asked Mike, kneeling down beside the chair.

"It's not the dumbbell," Rissa moaned through her tears. "I mean it *is* the dumbbell, but it's not." She let the tears fall from her eyes for a few minutes, until she noticed Mike's bewildered face. "My modeling contract is up in June," she told him. "And I didn't win the first prize."

"Sorry," he said, taking her hand. "But there will be other jobs. June is a long way off."

"What if there aren't any more? I don't want to live in a house with a bunch of . . . of dumbbells!" Tears swept over her once again. She knew she wasn't making sense to Mike. She'd tried to explain to him how she felt several times before, and he didn't seem to get it.

Living in a small house with four boys could be fun, but it was also chaotic. There were always smelly sneakers on the stairs, lacrosse sticks in the hallway, rusty bolts soaking in the sink. There were no floral-print wallpapers in the different rooms like in Marsha's house. No framed watercolors like there were in Sara's. Rissa described the decor in her house as being "Basic Boy."

For her, modeling had seemed like a door that could open into another, more elegant world. Modeling was her best hope for achieving the lovely, graceful life she dreamed about.

"You'll get more work," Mike assured her.

"You've already made . . . what? . . . a thousand dollars this year? That's great. Being the spokesperson is nothing."

Rissa sniffled and wiped her eyes. "You're right," she admitted. "It was just sitting on that stupid dumbbell as soon as I got the news that set me off. Sometimes I think of the future and it scares me."

"You'll always have me to rely on," he said, brushing a tear from her cheek. He leaned forward and kissed her lips.

"Rissa! The VCR is jammed!" Ralph cried, running into the room.

Rissa pulled away from Mike quickly. She groaned and rolled her eyes. When she saw Mike laugh, she laughed too. "I'm coming, I'm coming," she said as she pulled herself up out of the chair.

In the den, she found her thirteen-year-old brother Fred, who had come in through the back door a few minutes earlier, yanking on a tape cartridge that was sticking halfway out of the VCR. "This thing just started chewing up the tape," he said. "Now I can't even get it out." A final sturdy yank produced the tape.

"Dad is going to kill us if we bust the VCR," Rissa told him. She tried to insert the *Jaws* tape again. No luck. It simply wouldn't go in.

"Watch regular TV," she told her brothers as she snapped on the set. Shaking her head wearily, Rissa left the room and returned to Mike. "You're going to have to go when Marsha and Sara come," she told him. "We're making Marsha over into a presidential candidate." She went on to tell him about Marsha's candidacy.

"Why can't Marsha run as herself?" he asked.

"You don't understand how these things work,"

she said. "You have to present a clear-cut image to your public. Trust me. I'm in the business." She paused sadly. "Or at least I was."

"You still are," he said, wrapping his strong arms around her.

"I know," she said. "Modeling is just so important to me."

"More important than sports?" he asked as they walked into the living room.

"Maybe," she answered, considering it.

He faced her and put his arms around her waist. "More important than me?"

Rissa shook her head and smiled up at him. He leaned in close and pulled her to him. Their lips had barely touched when the doorbell rang.

"I don't believe this," sighed Rissa.

"I'll get it," said Mike.

A few seconds later Mike walked back into the living room. "There are two girls at your front door," he said, "and one of them is extremely unhappy."

Chapter Six

Marsha stormed into the living room behind Mike and threw herself down into a chair. "I didn't even want to come tonight," she announced irritably. "Sara made me."

"What's the matter?" asked Rissa, sitting up.

"She's upset because her mother might not let her go out with Bobby tomorrow," said Sara, stepping into the room.

"What does that have to do with your wanting to come here?" asked Rissa, bewildered.

"Because I knew you'd agree with my mother," she answered, gloomily.

"I think this is my cue to go look at Roger's car," said Mike, heading for the front hall.

"Chicken," shouted Rissa.

Mike left the girls alone in the living room. "I'm not happy that you're so upset," Rissa said to Marsha. "Is it definite?"

Marsha shook her head. "She was going to discuss it with my father tonight. Then he called and said he had to work late. I'm going to be so humiliated if I can't go. Bobby will think I'm making it up. Oh, I'll look like such an infant!"

"They'll probably end up letting you go," Sara said, trying to comfort her.

"There's nothing you can do about it now, anyway," Rissa said. "Let's go upstairs and work on your presidential image." They followed Rissa up the stairs to her long, narrow bedroom. Marsha sat down hard on the edge of the twin bed and folded her arms. "Okay, now tell me how I'm supposed to look."

Rissa reached into the top drawer of her dresser and pulled out a manila folder. When she had gotten home from school, Rissa had gone through old magazines and newspapers and pulled out photographs of women in politics. Rissa spread the photos out on her bed.

"I am not wearing my hair like Margaret Thatcher. I can tell you that right now," said Marsha, picking up the newspaper clipping of England's prime minister.

"Of course not," said Rissa. "But see how she dresses."

"Get off it!" Sara exclaimed. "You don't expect Marsha to wear those frumpy dresses!"

"No, but her dresses *are* simple and sensible. You have to seem like you have more important things on your mind than clothing," Rissa explained. "Yet you can't look sloppy."

"Can I model myself after Princess Di?" asked Marsha hopefully. "I wouldn't mind dressing like she does."

"First of all, you couldn't afford to dress like Princess Di. Second of all, she's not in politics," said Rissa. "She's a princess. It's her job to look pretty."

"Hey, you could wear a sari and lots of black eye makeup like the prime minister of Pakistan." Sara giggled. "She looks pretty neat."

"Very funny," said Marsha.

"Be serious," Rissa told Sara. "One thing I've noticed about all these women is that they have short hair."

"No!" Marsha gasped, clutching her long brown hair. "It's taken me forever to grow it out. I'm not touching it."

"Marsha!" Rissa insisted. "Look at these pictures. Do you see one woman with long hair?"

"But they're older than me," Marsha objected. "Besides, I don't have the money for a haircut." Rissa reached into her top drawer and pulled out a silver pair of sharp scissors. "Oh, no, you don't!" cried Marsha.

"Relax. I think you just need to take a few inches off—just so it falls to the end of your neck."

"Do you know what you're doing?" Sara asked Rissa skeptically.

"Sure. I'm the family haircutter," Rissa assured her.

"That's boys' hair," said Marsha.

"So? That doesn't mean I'm going to give you a boy's haircut."

Marsha eyed Rissa with a worried expression. "I guess an inch wouldn't be too bad. Just one inch—promise?"

"You'll barely notice it," said Rissa. "And it will make you appear to be more groomed."

"All right," Marsha agreed hesitantly.

"Go wash your hair," Rissa instructed her. "Use my white terry-cloth robe hanging on the back of the door when you're done."

Marsha went into Rissa's bathroom and undressed. She stepped into the tub and turned on the shower. On the shower shelf was a king-sized plastic bottle of generic-brand shampoo. Marsha poured some on her hair and immediately noticed that the shampoo had a smooth, oily texture.

She tried to work the shampoo into a lather, but nothing happened. It was no wonder that her parents never bought generic-brand items—they didn't work. She poured more shampoo onto her hair and worked it through the strands. There was still no lather.

Blaming it on the cheapness of the shampoo, she gave up and began to rinse . . . and rinse . . . and rinse. She realized her hair felt extremely oily and it wasn't coming clean.

Marsha shut off the water and pulled back the curtain.

Outside the door, she heard Fred shouting up the stairs. "Someone's on the phone for Marsha."

Bobby! That was Marsha's first thought. He hadn't had the nerve to cancel their date in person, but now he was doing it over the phone. He must have called her house first and her mother had said she was here.

Don't be so pessimistic, she scolded herself. *Maybe he just wants to change the time or something.* Marsha quickly put on Rissa's robe and grabbed a towel. She felt a strand of her hair. It was still oily. *Oh, well,* she thought, wrapping her hair in the towel, *maybe it will be all right when it dries.*

She opened the door just as Rissa was about to knock. "Phone for you," said Rissa.

"I know, I heard."

"You can take it in my father's room," said Rissa. "Only don't drip on the floor or do anything that will tip him off that you were there. No one's allowed in his room when he's not home, but Roger and I always go in and use the phone. There's no privacy in the kitchen."

Marsha stepped into Mr. Lupinski's plain, orderly

room. On his dresser she saw pictures of Rissa and the four boys at different ages. There was also a framed photo of a pretty woman with shining blue eyes and wavy blonde hair. Marsha had seen other pictures of Rissa's mother, but she'd never seen one in which the resemblance between Rissa and her mother was as strong as in this one.

She didn't have time to stop and study it, though. She picked up the tan phone on the nightstand. "Hello," she said, her voice anxious.

"You got it?" Fred spoke from the kitchen extension.

"Yes, you can hang up," said Marsha.

"You sure?" said Fred. "Maybe you'd like me to stay on the line."

"Don't be annoying, Fred," Marsha said tartly.

Fred chuckled and hung up. "Hello," Marsha said again, her heart in her throat. How was she supposed to act when he canceled their date?

"Hi, is this Marsha Kranton?" came a girl's voice.

Marsha sighed with relief. Bobby wasn't breaking their date, after all. "Yes," she said happily. "This is me—I mean, this is she. Who is this?"

"This is Sue Harmon."

"Hi, Sue," said Marsha. She was a girl in Marsha's honors math and gym classes. She was also a writer on the *Rosemont Reporter*, the school newspaper. Though they weren't close, they often talked during gym class which they both didn't like. Marsha considered her a friend. "What's up, Sue?"

"I hope you don't mind me bothering you at Rissa's house, but I'm going to write a story about you for the *Reporter* and I have to have it in by Monday."

"You mean because I'm running for class president?"

"Of course, silly."

"Sue, you sound different," said Marsha.

There was a pause, and then Sue sneezed loudly. "Must be this head cold," she said suddenly sounding very congested.

"Oh, yeah," said Marsha. "I didn't notice it before. You know, I'm so relieved it's you. I have a date tomorrow night and I was afraid you were him canceling."

"Wow! You have a date!"

"You don't have to sound so shocked!" said Marsha indignantly.

"Who with?"

"Bobby Turner," Marsha told her excitedly.

"Gee, he's cute. Why is he going out with you?"

"Sue!" Marsha cried.

"Sorry," she said in a stuffed-up voice. "Let me ask you some questions about the campaign. What made you think you could beat Doris?"

"I didn't even want to be in this thing," Marsha spoke into the phone confidentially. "Sara signed me up."

"Then you have no real hope of winning," said Sue, sounding as if she were writing things down.

"No, I do want to win," Marsha corrected her. "I have to save the school from that moron, Doris." Sue broke into a sudden fit of coughing on the other end. "Are you all right?" asked Marsha.

"Yes, yes, this cold is really getting bad," she answered in a choked voice. "What does Bobby Turner think of your running?"

"He says it's nothing more than a popularity contest. He's kind of a nonjoiner." Marsha thought for a moment. "Don't put any of this in the paper, okay, nothing about Sara signing me up or about Bobby."

"All right," Sue agreed.

Marsha smiled. "Maybe I'll promise to have the soccer field paved over and turned into a motorcycle racecourse. That would make him like the idea of my being president better," she joked.

Sue didn't laugh. "I was kidding," Marsha pointed out.

"Yes, of course. How silly of me." Sue went on to ask Marsha several questions about her candidacy. But they were odd questions. Marsha couldn't always figure out what they had to do with the campaign. "What subject do you hate the most?" Sue asked. Marsha was surprised that Sue didn't know she disliked gym the most. They spent practically every math class coming up with excuses they could use to be excused from gym.

"What would you like least about being class president?"

"My official answer is nothing. I think it would be a great challenge. But since we're friends I'll tell you. I'm nervous about whether or not I'll be able to handle it."

Sue's final question was the strangest. "As president of the class, what teacher would you like to see fired?"

"I can't answer that," Marsha objected.

"Okay, but just between us. Wouldn't you like to see Mrs. Haggler dumped?"

Mrs. Haggler was their gym teacher. She was really tough on the nonathletic girls, and Marsha was definitely nonathletic. "Between us, I'd like to see Mrs. Haggler abducted by gym-teacher–eating aliens."

"Me, too." Sue giggled. "That's about it. Thanks a lot."

"Did my answers sound all right?" Marsha asked

46

nervously. "Remember, don't mention anything about Bobby or Sara signing me up."

"I won't," she promised. "Bye."

Marsha hung up and sat on the bed. She was flattered that the *Reporter* was doing a story on her, but something about Sue sounded strange. The way she giggled, for one thing. Sue was not a giggler.

She got up, shaking off her misgivings. Everyone was entitled to giggle once in a while. Marsha smoothed out the rumpled spot on the bed where she'd been sitting and joined Rissa and Sara in Rissa's bedroom. "Sue Harmon is going to do a story on me," she told them.

"Great!" cried Rissa. "Free publicity."

"That's exciting," Sara agreed.

"What kind of weird shampoo is in your bathroom?" Marsha asked as she unwrapped the towel from her hair.

"It's basic no-name," Rissa replied. "Why?"

"It made my hair feel disgusting."

"Oh, excuse me. I'm sorry it's not Miss Froufrou Shampoo."

"I'm not being a snob." Marsha turned to Sara, who had been lying on the bed. "Feel my hair," she said.

Sara leaned forward and took a strand of hair. "Yuck-o!" she cried. "It feels like worms."

"See? I told you," said Marsha.

Rissa felt Marsha's hair. "Oooohhh. You're not kidding. I wonder what—" Rissa's eyes narrowed. "Fred!" she snarled.

"Fred?" asked Sara.

"Yeah, Fred. He's on this practical-joke kick." She left Sara and Marsha and went into the bathroom. She came back with the shampoo bottle and poured

47

some out onto her palm. "That's what I thought," she grumbled, sniffing the contents of the bottle. "It isn't shampoo. It's vegetable oil. Fred told me the kids at his camp did this all the time. It's a real pain to get out."

"What am I going to do!" Marsha wailed.

Chapter Seven

Marsha sighed deeply. "I hope you know what you're doing."

"Trust me," said Rissa as she knelt on the bed behind Marsha. She began snipping off the ends of Marsha's hair. "I'll trim it and then you can go wash the oil out."

"What if it doesn't come out?" moaned Marsha.

"It's got to come out," said Sara hopefully. "I mean, well, it must. Mustn't it?"

"It will, it will," said Rissa, sounding unsure despite her confident words. "And if it doesn't, I'll give you Fred's hair. I'll rip it right off his scalp."

"Oh, yuck, Rissa," said Sara.

"He gets me so mad with his dumb practical jokes," she said, snipping angrily at Marsha's hair.

"Hey, slow down. Don't cut too much," Marsha warned. Rissa cut more carefully, and after a while Marsha stopped worrying and began thinking about the campaign. "You know, today Nicky asked what issues I would be running on," she said. "I can't think of any issues."

"Well . . ." Sara considered. "What's important to you?"

"I don't know," Marsha replied. "I never thought about it."

"I'd like to see more importance put on girls' sports," said Rissa. "The boys get everything—new uniforms, bus transportation, pep rallies. Everyone acts as if their stuff is serious and ours is a joke."

"What could I do about it?" Marsha asked.

"I think the student council votes on how a special fund is spent every year," Sara suggested.

"Okay. That's one issue," said Marsha. "You know what bothers me? Study periods. I don't see why we're not allowed to go to the library for the whole period. It's a total waste of time to just sit there in class if you have a report you could be working on. And you can't do more than check out a book with those fifteen-minute passes they give. Maybe I could get that rule changed."

"Maybe," Rissa agreed, stepping back to see if Marsha's ends were even. "Hmmm," she mused. "Needs to be evened out on the right just a little."

"I don't see why we're not allowed to wear torn clothing to school," said Sara.

Marsha made a face at her. "Sorry, Sara. I am not campaigning on the right-to-wear-ripped-clothing issue. I don't think it would be a big vote-getter."

"It would get my vote," Sara said.

"I already have your vote."

"Don't keep wiggling your head," said Rissa, pushing Marsha's head forward. She combed her hair to the front and then pulled the ends forward to see if they were even. "Ugh, your hair feels so gross."

"Don't remind me," sighed Marsha. She sat quietly for a few moments. Her mind played back the events and conversations of the past few days. So much had happened. It annoyed Marsha that she always thought of clever, decisive things she should

50

have said after her conversations had ended. Now her head was filled with them.

I should have told Doris: "Yes, I am a nerd. It stands for Now Everyone Rejects Doris."

And I could have told Bobby: "I'm sorry you don't like my campaigning, but that's me. Take me as I am. I'm worth it."

Instead of whining, I should have said to my mother: "Either you trust me now or you never will."

I wish I had these real campaign issues in my mind when I spoke to Sue—

Suddenly Marsha jumped up. "That phone call!"

"Marsha!" Rissa shouted. "I could have cut your neck off. Are you crazy?"

"Sorry," Marsha said, "but I just realized something. That wasn't Sue Harmon on the phone. Sue went to her grandmother's funeral in Los Angeles. She left two days ago, on Wednesday. She said she wasn't coming back until Sunday night."

"Are you sure?" gasped Sara. "Maybe she came home early."

"Call her up to be sure," Rissa suggested. "Do you have her number?"

"No, but I know where she lives." The three girls went into Mr. Lupinski's bedroom and took the phone directory out from a shelf on the night table. They found Sue Harmon's number and Marsha dialed. Marsha listened impatiently to the ringing on the other end. Just as she was about to put down the receiver, a boy picked up and said, "Hello?"

"This is Marsha Kranton. Is Sue there?" Marsha asked, hopefully.

"Just a second," said the boy.

"Hi, Marsha," came Sue's voice.

"Hi," said Marsha. "Could you hold on a minute?'' She covered the mouthpiece with her hand. ''I guess I was wrong,'' Marsha whispered to Rissa and Sara. ''She's home.''

Feeling foolish, Marsha claimed that she was calling because she hadn't asked about the funeral before and she felt badly. ''The funeral was fine,'' said Sue. ''We came home early because they really didn't need Mom to do anything out there. But what do you mean you didn't ask about it before?''

''Before, when we talked on the phone,'' Marsha reminded her.

''I think you're cracking up, Kranton.'' Sue laughed. ''I haven't spoken to you since school three days ago.''

''Oh, yeah, well, maybe I am cracking up. See you Monday.'' Marsha put down the receiver. ''She didn't call me.''

''Then who was it?'' asked Sara.

''Who else?'' said Rissa.

''Doris,'' Marsha stated flatly.

''How could you fall for that?'' cried Rissa. ''Didn't you recognize her voice?''

''She disguised it. I knew something was fishy, but she said she had a cold.''

''Did you say anything revealing to her?'' Sara asked.

Marsha flopped back on Mr. Lupinski's bed. ''I told her everything. I told her you signed me up, I told her that Bobby thought it was a personality contest, I said I wasn't sure I could handle the job . . .''

''Brilliant, Marsha. Brilliant,'' said Rissa.

''I thought it was Sue. I could have trusted Sue,'' said Marsha. ''I feel really sick. I don't even want to think about what Doris will do with the information.''

52

"I'm sure we'll soon find out," said Rissa grimly.

"That little worm," Sara sneered. "She didn't even give you one day's peace before starting with her dirty tricks."

Rissa suddenly realized Marsha was lying on the bed. "Get up!" she cried. "You'll get grease all over my father's bedspread. He'll know we were in here for sure."

"Sorry," said Marsha, getting up. She and Rissa smoothed the spread.

"I could kill that Doris," said Marsha. "She has such a devious mind. Sometimes I wish I could think like—"

"Shhh!" Rissa interrupted. "I thought I heard my father's car pull in." She cocked her head and listened. "That *is* his car. I wonder why he's back so soon."

Chapter Eight

The girls stood on the staircase waiting for Mr. Lupinski to come through the front door. They heard a jangling of keys from outside the door, and seconds later Mr. Lupinski, followed by a delicate, dark-haired woman, stepped into the front hall.

"Hi, Mary," Rissa said to the woman. "You're home early, Dad. Is everything okay?"

"Everything is great," he answered.

Rissa seized the opportunity, and mentioned the broken VCR. Better to get it over with now, she thought. "It wasn't really anyone's fault," she told him. Then she held her breath, waiting for him to explode.

His eyes briefly flashed and then became calm. "Those things are always breaking," he muttered as Fred, Ralph, and Harry emerged from the kitchen.

"Why are you home so soon?" asked Fred.

"All of you come sit down. I have something to tell you," said Mr. Lupinski.

"We'll wait upstairs," said Sara, heading back up.

"Yes, yes, please, just give us a few minutes," said Mr. Lupinski.

"This is too weird," Rissa whispered to Marsha and Sara.

54

"Good luck," said Sara as she and Marsha headed up the stairs.

When the family was seated in the living room—the four kids sprawled out on two couches and Mr. Lupinski and Mary standing in the middle of the room—Mr. Lupinski took Mary by the hand. "We were so excited about our news that we came right home to tell you. We didn't even bother to order dinner. Mary has agreed to be my wife," he announced, a wide grin covering his usually serious face.

Rissa heard his words, but they didn't sink in. It was as if they were only sounds coming from his mouth and they had no meaning. She sat there staring blankly at her father.

"Congratulations," said Fred, rising and shaking his father's hand. He gave Mary a kiss on the cheek.

The twins awkwardly followed. They each hugged Mary. Rissa knew the boys liked Mary. Why shouldn't they? she thought. Mary treated them like little princes—never expecting them to do anything around the house and practically applauding at everything they said.

All eyes turned to Rissa, awaiting her response. "When are you getting married?" she asked quietly.

"I wanted to be married by a friend of mine, who's a priest," said Mary. "He's supposed to come into town from Italy at the end of the month. So if he agrees to marry us, we'll do it then."

"This month?" asked Rissa, her voice cracking in surprise. "That's only three weeks away."

"We'll have to see what can be arranged," said Mary. "But even if Father Benzoni can't perform the ceremony, we want to get married soon. After all, we're not exactly young kids anymore."

Rissa noticed a worried look in Mary's dark eyes, and knew that she needed Rissa to say something reassuring. The words "Welcome to the family" or "I'm so happy for you" seemed to be what she was waiting for, but Rissa couldn't say them. She wasn't sure they would be sincere. She didn't know *how* she felt about this news.

"That's great!" said Fred, responding to the awkwardness of the moment.

That helped relieve the tension, but Rissa knew Mary and her father were still waiting for a response from her. "I hope you'll both be very happy," she said, getting up from the couch and forcing her lips into a tight smile.

"Thank you," said Mary. She leaned toward Rissa as though she expected a kiss, but Rissa pretended she didn't notice. All she wanted was to get away from her father and Mary. She needed some time alone to sort out her feelings.

"Well . . ." said Mr. Lupinski, looking around at his family, "that's my news. We're all going to make Mary very happy here, aren't we?" He made the last statement while looking pointedly at Rissa.

Rissa nodded while her brothers shouted their yesses. Her father and Mary smiled and said they were starving. "I can whip up some dinner for everyone," said Mary. "You kids hungry?"

The boys nodded, but Rissa saw her chance to escape. "I ate and I should get back to my friends," she said with unusual primness.

"Do you feel all right, Rissa?" Mary asked, obviously genuinely concerned. "You look very pale. I hope this news hasn't upset you."

"No," Rissa lied politely. "I do have a little headache, though."

"Take a nice hot shower," Fred suggested. "That always makes me feel better when I have a headache."

"That's right. I almost forgot!" shouted Rissa. She grabbed Fred roughly by the arm. "What's the big idea of putting vegetable oil in the shampoo bottle? I'm going to kill you."

Fred chuckled wickedly. Rissa shook him hard. "Hey, cut it out!" he cried. "It was just a joke."

"Some joke!" Rissa shouted. "I ought to pop you one right in the—"

"Clarissa Jean!" Mr. Lupinski barked. Rissa shot him a defiant glare and then backed down. "I'm sorry, but Fred played a mean trick on Marsha."

Fred let out a hoot of laughter. "I thought she looked kind of strange when I saw her on the stairs."

Rissa shoved Fred hard on the shoulder. "Poor Marsha was all upset."

"How was I supposed to know she was going to wash her hair here?" Fred yelped, rubbing his shoulder. "It was meant for you."

"That's enough, the two of you," said Mr. Lupinski.

"I have to go upstairs," Rissa said sullenly. She ran straight up the staircase, down the hall, and into her bedroom. She was glad Marsha and Sara were staying over. At least they'd understand her.

When she got to her room she was greeted by a stony-faced Marsha. "I thought you said you could cut hair!" she snapped at Rissa.

Rissa felt her stomach tighten. It did look horrible. Somehow when her hair had been wetter, the oil made it all seem so smooth and even. But now that it was drying, little wisps of frizz were popping out all over. Her cut wasn't lying as evenly as Rissa had thought—especially in the back. The ends were choppy

57

and fell at noticeably different lengths. She didn't understand it. Marsha's hair had looked fine . . . before it began to dry. "It's just the oil," said Rissa hopefully. "Once you wash it, it will look fine."

"It won't look fine!" hissed Marsha. "You butchered my hair."

"I'll even it out, that's all," Rissa said.

"Oh, no, you don't!" shouted Marsha. "I'm not letting you near this hair. If Sara hadn't told me, I'd be walking around with a big chunk of hair missing from the back. I think you did this deliberately because you don't want my date with Bobby to go well tomorrow. I know you don't like him, but I never thought you'd do something this mean."

Rissa's jaw dropped open. "That is such a lie! You're the one who jumped up in the middle of the haircut."

"Marsha, you're just upset," Sara said, trying to make peace.

"Of course I'm upset. I'm running for class president. Everyone is going to be looking at me. And, I finally get a date with a boy I'm wild about, and *she* goes and ruins my hair!"

Rissa's face went red with fury. "Marsha, I can't believe how selfish you are. My whole life is falling apart and you're whining about your hair."

"What happened?" asked Sara.

"My father is engaged to Mary. They're getting married in three weeks!"

"That's great," said Sara. "At least, I think it is. Isn't it, Rissa?"

"I think it's a lot more important problem than your hair," Rissa said to Marsha.

"What do you mean, a problem?" cried Marsha.

"That's not a problem. That's good news. You're supposed to be happy about stuff like that."

"You are so insensitive!" said Rissa. "I'm going to have to live with a person who's practically a stranger and you're babbling on about your hair."

"Oh, sorry," said Marsha sarcastically. "I guess I shouldn't have said anything about it. The next time you destroy my looks I won't be so selfish as to mention it."

"Please don't mention it! Listen, I don't care if you ever speak to me about anything again," said Rissa angrily.

"That's fine with me!" snarled Marsha, heading out of the bedroom. "I think I'll be going home now." She grabbed her clothing from Rissa's bed and stormed into the bathroom.

"You don't mean that, about not wanting to speak to Marsha anymore," Sara pleaded with Rissa.

"Yes, I do," said Rissa, glaring at the closed bathroom door.

A minute later, Marsha came out of the bathroom, her oily hair pushed back off her forehead. "Some friend you are," she said.

"Don't worry about it," Rissa shot back, "because as far as I'm concerned, our friendship is over."

Chapter Nine

Marsha studied her reflection in the mirror and frowned. It was Saturday afternoon and she should have been happy about her date. She was—but her fight with Rissa had put a pall over her good mood.

This was so unfair. She was going out with Bobby. The new haircut she'd gotten that afternoon took care of the hair problem. It was a little shorter than she would have liked, but the chin-length style was nice for a change. But the Rissa problem made her feel awful.

Could Rissa really mean that their friendship was over? They'd been friends since grammar school. It seemed impossible. Still, Rissa hadn't called. Maybe she was serious.

I can't think about that now, Marsha said to herself. Bobby would be over in a little while and she didn't want to seem gloomy and depressed when he arrived.

Friday night, after she'd come home from Rissa's house, Marsha's parents gave her their permission to go out with Bobby. They did, however, have their reservations and conditions. No motorcycle! That was number one and they must have repeated it a hundred times. Also, they were to go to the Rosemont Twin Theater, which was within walking distance. And Marsha had to be in by eleven o'clock. Sharp!

Marsha wasn't about to argue with them. She was just glad they were allowing her to go out with Bobby.

She practiced smiling in the mirror. *You look ridiculous,* she told herself. She decided to wear a neutral expression—with a touch of a smile in her eyes—when Bobby arrived.

Pushing back the front sides of her hair, she continued to study her new haircut. Once her mother saw the terrible job Rissa had done on Marsha's hair, it didn't take much to convince her to pay for a haircut. Marsha took the twenty dollars her mother gave her and practically ran down to the Sunshine Haircutters on Rosemont Avenue.

She fluffed her new chin-length cut. She hadn't intended to have it cut so short, but the hairdresser had said it was the only way she could even out all the ends. She liked the cut, though. It made her hazel eyes look much larger, and it gave her hair a healthy bounce.

At least Rissa would be happy that she now had presidential-style short hair, thought Marsha. Then she remembered that she and Rissa were no longer friends.

Marsha was still angry at Rissa. Sometimes Rissa thought she knew everything.

She stepped onto her bed, trying to see her entire reflection in the mirror. After rejecting several outfits, she had settled on blue jeans, a long blue sweater, and a pair of short leather boots. She jumped off the bed and dug through her top drawer and found a pair of silver hoop earrings. She slipped them onto her pierced ears.

"Oh, I couldn't agree more," she said into the mirror, pretending she was talking to Bobby. As she spoke, she tossed back her hair, admiring the shine of the earrings.

She went to her closet and took out her brand-new faded denim jacket. She'd spent months saving her allowance money for it. She ripped off the tags and slipped it on. It was impossible to be mistaken for a twerp while wearing a jacket like this. It made her feel cool instantly.

Suddenly an engine roared in the driveway. Marsha raced down the stairs, terrified that her father would already be in the driveway saying something embarrassing to Bobby. She got downstairs just in time. Her father was heading straight for the front door.

"I thought you told that young man you were not allowed on his motorcycle," said her father, rubbing his hand agitatedly across the top of his bald head.

"I'm going to tell him, this second," Marsha replied quickly. "I'll handle it. Please don't say anything, Daddy. Please."

Marsha ran out and met Bobby in the driveway. He pulled off his helmet and smiled at her. "I brought you an extra helmet," he said, gesturing at the helmet strapped on the back of the bike.

Marsha knew just what she was going to say. She'd been practicing all day. "That's great, Bobby. But why don't we walk over to the Rosemont Twin. It's so nice out and I'd love to see that new movie with Cher that's playing there." She said it all in one rush and then studied his face to see how it had gone over.

His eyes lit with laughter. "Your parents having a fit over the bike?" he asked.

"How did you know?" Marsha admitted.

"Hey, my parents have a fit over this thing every day," he said, climbing off the motorcycle. "Can I leave it back by your garage?"

"Sure," Marsha said, her voice filled with relief.

He walked the bike back into the yard and then joined her in front. "Your hair looks nice that way," he commented.

"Thanks." Marsha smiled. "Come on inside. Don't mind my father. He's kind of a pain sometimes," she warned him. They walked into the living room. She stifled a smile when she saw her father sitting on the sofa with a newspaper in front of him. He was acting like he had been casually sitting there all along.

Her mother came downstairs. Marsha was relieved that both her parents were behaving reasonably well. They simply said hello and reminded Marsha to be home by eleven.

Marsha and Bobby talked about school as they walked toward the theater. Inevitably, the subject of the campaign came up. "I thought you weren't interested in these popularity contests," Bobby said. "That's what you said in class. Besides, what will it do for you?"

Not wanting to admit that she did want to be popular, Marsha wasn't sure how to answer. "I don't know. Sara roped me into it, but now it seems like it might be fun."

"Riding a motorcycle is fun. Going to a movie is fun. Running for class president sounds like work to me."

"Oh, I'd better tell you now," Marsha said. "You might hear your name mentioned in this campaign." She told him all about Doris's phony phone call and how she'd mentioned his name. "I'm not sure what she's planning, but I want you to be prepared."

Bobby sighed. "I don't care. But if you weren't involved with this you wouldn't have to deal with stupid stuff like that."

"You really think I'm a jerk for doing this, don't you?" said Marsha.

"You? No. Never," he said. "No, I guess I just don't go in for this civic jazz. I'm more of an outsider when it comes to school."

"But do you like it that way?" she dared to ask.

"Sure," he said without hesitation.

Marsha admired his certainty, but she knew she would never be content to think of herself as an outsider. He seemed to feel no need for approval. She wished she felt that way, but she didn't.

From her seat next to him in the theater, she could smell a mixture of the leather of his jacket and the faint spicy smell of his cologne.

The movie was funny. Marsha found herself laughing hard—so hard that tears rolled down her cheeks. Aware that her mascara was running, she excused herself to go to the ladies' room.

She washed her face and was about to go back to her seat when she spotted Doris and Craig Lawrence buying popcorn in the lobby. Doris went out with Craig whenever there was no one she found more interesting to go out with. Craig was so in love with her that he took whatever Doris dished out.

Squaring her shoulders, Marsha intended to walk past them as if she hadn't seen them.

"Hey, Marsha," Craig called. Marsha always suspected that Craig felt a little guilty toward her after the way he'd treated her last spring. He'd stood her up for the June dance at the last minute so that he could go with Doris. For whatever reason, he never let her pass without a cheery "Hey, Marsha."

"Hello, Craig," Marsha said politely.

Beside him Doris stood tossing popcorn into her mouth one by one. Even the way she ate popcorn, holding each piece between her long pink fingernails, Marsha found irritating. The sneer Doris was directing at Marsha wasn't helping, either. She hadn't planned on speaking to Doris, but suddenly the thought that Doris still believed she'd fooled Marsha on the phone was too much for her.

"That was a very funny little joke the other night, Doris," said Marsha. "You didn't fool me for an instant, though. Nothing I said to you was true."

"Tell that to the tape recorder," Doris replied, unruffled.

"The tape . . . the . . . You sneak!" cried Marsha.

"I think I'll be going back to my seat," said Craig, clearly wanting no part of this scene.

The two girls ignored him as he drifted away, back into the theater. "You had no right!" Marsha huffed.

"All's fair in love and war, hon," Doris said with a smirk.

"Don't you call me hon," said Marsha, enraged. "You are a creepy little nothing, Doris. And if you think you can intimidate me out of running against you, you're wrong. There is nothing you can do to make me feel small and stupid. Because I will never be as small and stupid as you are." Marsha breathed hard with anger, but she felt great. For once she had found the words she wanted while the conversation was going on. She felt exultant.

"Oh, yeah?" said Doris. "Well, here's a little something from that moron—as you called me—Doris Gaylord." As she spoke, Doris dumped her entire large-sized buttered popcorn over Marsha's head. Then she turned sharply and went back into the theater.

"Oh! . . . Oh! . . ." fumed Marsha. She didn't know what to do. If she'd had popcorn she would have thrown it back. But she didn't have any. And before she could do anything, Doris had disappeared. She had to hand it to Doris. She was a master at making someone feel small and stupid.

She picked some popcorn out of the collar of her shirt. She pulled some more out of her hair. *Leave it to Doris to order extra butter,* she thought wretchedly. Although most of it was on the floor, a lot of popcorn was still in Marsha's hair, in her collar, attached to her sweater.

As if things weren't bad enough, at that moment Bobby came through the theater door into the lobby. He studied her for half a second. "That's what I like to see," he joked. "A girl who really gets into her food. Looks like you're enjoying that popcorn."

"Oh, Bobby," Marsha wailed, picking popcorn off her sweater. There was a tingle of rising tears under her eyes, but she was determined not to embarrass herself further by crying.

"What happened?" he asked, growing serious.

"I told Doris off about that phone call. And this was her response."

"I guess you scared her, huh?" He laughed.

"Stop it," she said, smiling despite herself. "This isn't funny."

"Hey, I'm not going to say anything," he said, holding up his hands. "You're the one who wanted to tangle with this Doris person. Want me to go inside and pulverize her for you?"

"No." Marsha smiled. "I *would* like to get out of here, though."

66

"No problem," he said, heading for the front door. "But if I take you for something to eat, can I trust you not to dive into it?"

"I promise," said Marsha. "As long as we don't run into Doris again."

"Hey, think of it this way. At least she wasn't eating pizza," he said as they walked out into the fresh night air.

They stopped at a diner on the way home and had hamburgers and sodas. "I've been wanting to ask you out since school began," Bobby admitted, poking the ice cubes in his soda with his straw.

"You should have," Marsha said shyly.

He looked at her with surprise. "Yeah? I thought maybe you liked the more intellectual type, so I wasn't sure what to do."

"Well, I'm happy you asked," Marsha said, trying not to blush.

"Me too," he replied.

He held her hand on the way home and talked about his family. He had two older brothers. "They're real jocks though," he said. "I don't have a lot in common with them."

"Well, here it is—the old house," Marsha said as they approached her front walk. She suddenly felt awkward at this parting moment.

"And I got you home fifteen minutes early," said Bobby, walking Marsha to the front door.

"You'll definitely score big points with my dad for that one," said Marsha.

"Good," he said dreamily, stooping toward her. The next thing Marsha knew, she was in his arms and they were kissing. She felt his strength as he held her close. She staggered back a step toward the door when he let her go.

"I can never resist a girl who smells like melted butter," he said with a gentle smile.

Marsha nodded and smiled back. "I'm glad I wore this fragrance then."

"I'll see you Monday, in school," he said.

"I had a nice time. Thanks," she said. Marsha watched as he went and got his bike. She waved one last time as he pulled out down the driveway.

The way she felt about Bobby was the way she'd always imagined it would be when she fell in love. She knew now that her feelings for Craig had been just a silly crush. And her relationship with Jim had been friendship, not romance. But this was the blood-rushing, heart-pounding, thrilled-to-death real thing.

Her parents were up watching TV when she went inside. "How was your date?" her mother asked.

"Completely and totally wonderful." Marsha sighed happily.

Chapter Ten

On Sunday, Sara came over. They sat in Marsha's bedroom and worked on more posters for her campaign. Marsha told her about her encounter with Doris.

"That's so awful," said Sara. "Didn't you want to punch her right in the mouth?"

"I wanted to, but first of all she disappeared too fast. And second of all, if I did, you know she'd tell the whole school that I attacked her."

"*She* attacked *you*," Sara insisted.

"Yeah, but it sounds ridiculous going around telling people she dumped popcorn on me. It's not the same, somehow. If I complained it would make me sound like a wimp."

"What did Bobby do?" Sara asked.

"He made it seem like it was no big deal—like it was funny almost—which I suppose it might have been if it had happened to someone else." Marsha went on to tell Sara all about her date.

"He sounds neat," Sara said, when Marsha had finished giving her every detail of the evening, right down to the patty melt with extra cheese that Bobby had ordered at the diner.

"And then he kissed me at the door," Marsha confided.

"Yeah? So, was it great?" asked Sara, curiously.

"It was . . . indescribable," Marsha said dreamily.

"Nicky says he's a good guy," said Sara. "He sees him a lot since he hangs out with Stingo's brother, Stu. Rissa will change her mind about Bobby when she hears that he was so nice to you after Doris slimed you with popcorn butter."

"I don't care what Rissa thinks," said Marsha, looking up from the poster she'd been intently working on.

"Don't be that way," Sara urged her. "Rissa's real upset about her father getting married. Give her a break."

"Why is she upset?" asked Marsha. "Mary seems nice."

"It's going to be a big change for her," Sara pointed out. "And you know Rissa isn't a hundred percent crazy about Mary. She thinks she's too old-fashioned."

Marsha shrugged coldly. "That's not my problem. My problem is winning this campaign. Now I don't have a campaign manager."

"You and Rissa will be friends again by Monday," said Sara.

"Maybe," said Marsha, still feeling stubborn toward Rissa. Deep down, though, she knew Sara was right. She wasn't *that* angry, and Rissa probably wasn't either.

Marsha got to school early on Monday with a bundle of oaktag posters rolled under her arm. Sara had taken the other bunch. Marsha saw a few of them already hanging, so she knew Sara was putting them up as well.

Marsha taped the posters up around the school, being careful not to put them too close to Doris's more professional-looking ones. She was busy putting up posters until just before the first bell. When it rang, she grabbed her books and hurried to homeroom.

Slowly, Marsha was becoming aware that her campaign had given her a new status. Today kids turned and smiled at her when she entered. She noticed two girls in the far corner of the room whispering and looking her way. She didn't know them well, but now one of the girls caught her eye and mouthed the words "Love your hair."

Marsha smiled and mouthed back, "Thanks." It was working already! Suddenly people she never talked to before were aware of her. They were talking about her, and even noticing her hair. It felt good.

She looked over at Doris, who was turned around in her seat, laughing with Heather and the two boys on either side of her. Their eyes locked for a second, but Doris turned away, pretending to take no notice of Marsha.

After taking attendance, Mrs. Ritter was called out of class by another teacher. As soon as the door closed behind her, the class became noisy.

Gary Herman, the boy sitting next to Doris, got up and went over to the window. He opened it and peered down toward the ground. The class was on the first floor, so it was only several feet to the ground. "Hey, I'm out of here," he called to his friend, Tony Harris, who was sitting on the other side of Doris. "Want to come?"

Tony joined Gary and the two of them hopped out the window just as Mrs. Ritter returned. The teacher scowled. "What's so funny?" she asked, sensing that something was up. She looked around the room.

71

"Where are Tony and Gary?" she asked after a moment. No one said anything.

"I know they were here," she insisted.

"They went to the bathroom," Doris said, covering for them.

Mrs. Ritter looked skeptical, but at that moment the bell rang for homeroom. "If anyone sees Gary, tell him I received a message for him. Have him come see me."

The class filed out the door and into the hallway. Marsha was about to walk through the door, when Mrs. Ritter called to her. She turned and went up to the teacher's desk.

"Marsha, I noticed your posters," Mrs. Ritter said. "It's not a big deal, but Mrs. Haggler said to ask you not to put any of them on the gym door. She's funny that way."

"Okay," said Marsha. "I'll take those down. How do you think they look?"

Mrs. Ritter suggested she put her picture on some of them and described different ways she could do it inexpensively. As she spoke, Marsha noticed a note on her desk. It said: *Gary Herman. Call father at hospital. Very important.*

Marsha lost track of what Mrs. Ritter was saying. What if this was an emergency and no one could find Gary all day long? She didn't know what to do. She didn't want to rat on him. On the other hand, what if someone in his family was sick—even dying?

"Mrs. Ritter," Marsha interrupted her teacher. "I think I know where Gary is." She felt guilty telling her teacher how he had cut out, but what if he never got the message? That would be even worse. "The kids usually hang out down at the Rosemont diner

72

and have breakfast when they cut out," she said. "Maybe someone could look for him there."

"Thank you, dear," said Mrs. Ritter, frowning. "I'll send Mr. Ames over to look for him."

A chill ran down Marsha's spine. Mr. Ames was the dean of discipline and he was not very popular with the students. "I didn't want to get him in trouble," Marsha said. "I just noticed the note there on your desk and it seemed that it might be important."

"You did the right thing, Marsha," said Mrs. Ritter. "I don't know what this is about, but it does say hospital on it."

Marsha left homeroom and found Sara waiting for her out in the hall. "What did Mrs. Ritter want?" she asked.

"She just wanted to tell me something about moving my posters away from the gym."

"Oh. Listen, I was talking to Rissa just now. She feels bad about what happened. Why don't the two of you make up," Sara urged her.

Marsha looked at her friend, knowing that Sara hated being in the middle. And the fight did seem pretty stupid. "Yeah, okay," said Marsha absently.

"You don't seem very positive about it," Sara observed.

"It's not that," said Marsha. "I guess I'll talk to Rissa later. I'm worried because I just told Mrs. Ritter what Gary did."

"What did he do?" Sara asked.

Marsha explained what had happened. "I thought there might have been an emergency in his family," she said, knitting her brows into a worried scowl. "I hope I did the right thing, Sara."

73

Chapter Eleven

Sara went into her house after school that afternoon and plopped down on the living room couch. The house was cool and quiet. Both her parents worked in Manhattan and wouldn't be home for another two and a half hours. It would be at least another hour before Elaine came home and started singing those awful scales.

Sara usually wasn't home this early. She generally went to Marsha's or Rissa's or practiced with the band. But today Nicky had left a note on her locker saying that practice was canceled because he had a dentist appointment and Stingo was making up a math test. Sara didn't feel much like singing today anyway. She needed quiet time to think.

Marsha and Rissa's feud was getting to her. She'd hoped they'd patch it up by lunchtime, but Rissa had gone to a girls' sports club meeting. After school Marsha had been talking to Bobby Turner at her locker. So things remained the same as they'd been the day before.

That was another reason Sara was home. She didn't want to appear partial by going to one girl's house and not the other's.

She stretched out on the couch and listened to the gentle ticking of the antique clock on the mantel. Her mind began drifting. She imagined herself on stage at a big arena with Nicky and the Eggheads—imagined the crowd going wild. She saw Nicky playing his sax and smiling warmly at her as he finished his solo. She smiled back and then belted out the rest of the song while the audience stood on their seats, rocking to the music.

The sound of the doorbell jolted her from her enjoyable daydream. "Who could this be?" she muttered, heading for the door. When she opened it she saw Nicky leaning up against the stoop railing. "Hi," she said. One look at his face told her that something was wrong. "What's the matter?"

"It shows, huh." He laughed sadly, coming into the house.

"Yeah, it shows all over your face," she replied, worried. "What happened?"

Nicky sat on the couch and leaned forward, pressing his hands down on his knees. An agitated expression played across his face. "I don't know how to say this."

Sara inhaled sharply. Was he breaking up with her? "What? Just tell me," she said, forcing herself to stay calm.

"I'm leaving Rosemont."

His words hit Sara like a fist. "Leaving Rose— What do you mean? For how long?"

"I don't know," he said. "My dad's business is sending him to Hong Kong to set up an office. Either I go there with him, or I go back to living with my mom in London. But no matter what, it means I have to go. I've known about it for a couple of weeks, but I was hoping it wouldn't happen. That's why I've been so down lately."

Sara was stunned. She couldn't imagine his not

75

being there anymore. This couldn't be happening. "They can't just take you out of school!" Sara cried. "Haven't you been bounced around enough already? It's totally unfair!"

"Sara, please calm down," he said helplessly.

"I can't calm down!" she shouted as tears filled her eyes. "What about me? What about you and me?"

He stood and put his arms around her. She buried her face in his chest and let her hot tears soak his shirt. She had always thought the term heartache was another way of saying sadness. Now she knew differently. She had a real pain in her chest surrounded by a genuine, awful, dull aching.

Sara put her arms around Nicky and grabbed the material of his blue sweatshirt in her fists. "You can't go," she wept. "I won't let you go."

He tightened his embrace and held her until her tears subsided. "What are we going to do?" she said finally, looking up at him with tear-drenched eyes.

He brushed the wet ends of her hair from her cheek and sighed. "I wish I were older. Then I could stay wherever I pleased."

They sat beside each other on the couch. "Go to London, not Hong Kong," said Sara. "It's not as far away."

"I know, but I never did get along with my mom's new husband. And Hong Kong would be more exciting. Me and my dad are just starting to get close. I'd hate to leave him now."

"But it's on the other side of the world! Maybe I could find a way to visit you in London, but I could never ever afford the airfare to Hong Kong!"

They fell silent. The ticking of the clock seemed

very loud to Sara. "How soon do you have to leave?" she forced herself to ask.

Nicky entwined his fingers with hers. "In two weeks," he answered with a catch in his voice. "Another guy was all set to go and he backed out at the last minute. Of course my dad was willing. He says it's a real break for his career. He's completely ecstatic about it."

"At least someone's happy," Sara muttered.

"You'll write to me, won't you?" Nicky asked.

Sara's eyes opened wider. "Of course! How can you even ask that question? I'll write to you every single day. Twice a day! You don't have to write me that often, I'll understand if you don't. But all I'll be doing is thinking about you, anyway, so I might as well write."

A small, sad smile formed on Nicky's lips. "That's nice of you to say," he said.

"It's true!" cried Sara.

"I know you mean it, but I've moved before. Your friends write a lot at first, then the letters get fewer and fewer. Then they stop altogether. It's the way it goes. I'll write to you, though. Don't worry about that."

"Don't worry about me, either," Sara assured him. "Nicky," she said after another long silence, "do you think this is the end of us?"

"I guess we'll survive," he replied.

"No, I mean of us. Of you and me as an us."

He thought about that question for a moment. "Not if we were really meant to be an us," he answered quietly.

Sara wrapped her arms around his neck. "We were—we are. I know we are. We'll be together again." She gazed up into his handsome, unhappy face and kissed him hard on the lips. He kissed her back with equal force. Sara shut her eyes and tried to memorize the feel of his lips on hers.

The sound of the front door opening made them jump apart. "Anybody home?" Elaine called from the front hall.

"Me and Nicky," Sara called back quickly. She knew Elaine would remind her that she wasn't allowed to have any boys in the house when her parents weren't home. She and Elaine always squabbled, but Sara wasn't in the mood to fight with her now.

Elaine came into the living room looking annoyed. "Sara, you know—" To Sara's surprise, her sister stopped herself. She never thought of Elaine as being particularly perceptive about other people's feelings, but something on Sara's and Nicky's faces must have told her this was serious. "You guys better go outside before Mom and Dad get home," she said simply, heading up the stairs.

Sara and Nicky went outside for a walk. They talked about how they would write and worked out a plan so they could be together for the summer. They decided that Nicky would apply for work at Hemway Park. Sara had worked there last summer, in the parking lot. "Stingo's parents might let me stay with them—at least for the summer," Nicky said hopefully.

By the time they reached the Rosemont Avenue Park, they were feeling a little better. "The time will go by quickly, and we can even talk on the phone sometimes," said Sara, sitting on one of the swings. "I'll save all my money for phone calls."

He took the swing beside her. "I'll miss you the most, and then second to that, I'll miss playing with the band."

"So will I," said Sara, digging the toes of her sneakers in the dirt.

"What do you mean?" Nicky asked. "You don't have to leave the Eggheads because I won't be there."

"The band isn't going on without you," said Sara, shocked that he would think such a thing. "There's nobody strong enough to hold it together. Stingo's too disorganized. And I like Eric and Sam and all, but—face it—they're followers."

"What about you?" he said.

Sara let out a hoot of laughter. "I know the guys like me, but they wouldn't listen to me. Besides, I couldn't go out and get jobs and write songs and make sure everyone showed up for practice the way you do. You're the head honcho. That's why the group is called Nicky and the Eggheads, remember?"

"That's flattering, but I'd hate to see the group fall apart on my account."

"Without you, there will be no group," said Sara.

They walked home without saying much. Nicky left her at her front door and walked away with his hands in his pockets and his head bent down toward the sidewalk.

When Sara got inside, she asked to be excused from dinner. She didn't feel much like eating. Instead, she went upstairs and called Rissa. "Hi, it's me," she said glumly when Rissa picked up. "Ask me what's new."

"What's new?" asked Rissa.

"The world is an unfair, crummy, horrible place, that's what," Sara answered.

"What's the matter, Sara?" Rissa asked.

"Nicky is moving because his father has been transferred."

There was silence on Rissa's end. "I can't believe it," she said, finally. "Is it definite?"

"It sounded definite."

"That's horrible. How do you feel?"

Sara opened her mouth to describe how she felt, but there was a lump in her throat and she couldn't speak.

"Are you there? Are you okay?" Rissa asked.

"I don't think I want to talk about it, okay?" Sara said in a choked voice.

"Okay," Rissa said. "Are you sure?"

Sara bit her lip and tried not to cry. "Uh-huh. Talk to you tomorrow." She hung up and wiped her eyes. She decided it was better not to talk about it. She'd tell Marsha tomorrow.

After reading a few chapters of *Jane Eyre,* she went to sleep—even though it was only eight o'clock. She woke up again when the red numbers of her digital clock read one o'clock A.M.

Sara sat up in bed, her eyes slowly adjusting to the dark. Nicky's leaving was going to change her whole life. She was losing her two greatest loves—Nicky and singing with the band. She knew she was right about the Eggheads. They were sure to drift apart without Nicky.

Then another unpleasant thought occurred to her. She'd been so upset, she'd forgotten all about Marsha's campaign. *How am I going to tell Marsha that we can't play at her pep rally?* she wondered miserably. And she tossed and turned the rest of the night.

Chapter Twelve

On Tuesday, Marsha woke up full of energy. She was anxious to get to school and start her campaign. Although the thought of Doris's next action made her stomach flip a bit, she knew she had to be there to combat it. She felt like a soldier going into battle—nervous, but energized.

Marsha dressed and went to the kitchen. "You're up early," commented her mother, who was sleepily putting coffee into the coffeemaker. "It usually takes at least three wake-up calls to rouse you."

"I have to campaign today," she told her mother.

"Good, now you have time for a decent breakfast for a change," said her mother.

"Nope," said Marsha, grabbing an apple from the refrigerator. "I want to get there early. I don't want Doris pulling any stunts while I'm not around."

"Don't let that girl rattle you," said her mother.

"I won't," Marsha said, hoping she'd be able to keep her cool with Doris. She kissed her mother on the cheek and hurried out the door.

Marsha got to school a half hour before the first bell. She walked through the quiet halls toward her locker.

When she reached her locker, she was surprised to see Sara standing in front of it. One look at her face told Marsha that Sara was upset about something. "Why are you here so early? What's the matter?"

"I have to tell you something, and I was so nervous about telling you that I got up at five o'clock this morning." Sara yawned. "I've been up for so long it seems like it should be noon. I didn't know what else to do with myself, so I just came to school."

"What do you have to tell me?" asked Marsha, worried.

"The band isn't going to be able to play at your rally," she blurted out.

"Why not?" Marsha demanded.

Sara told her about Nicky having to leave. "That's what's been making him so gloomy lately?" said Marsha. Sara nodded. "That stinks," Marsha sympathized. "How are you feeling?"

"Rotten," said Sara. She leaned up against the locker as though she really needed it to keep her standing.

"I'll bet," Marsha said. "But why can't the rest of you play without him?"

"Because we can't!" Sara said matter-of-factly.

"Okay, you don't have to be so touchy," said Marsha. "I was counting on you to help me out, that's all."

"Well, I'm sorry, Marsha. I feel terrible but we just can't do it."

Just then Nicky came down the hall. "I guess he couldn't sleep either," said Sara. Marsha looked at Nicky and had to agree. There were dark circles under his eyes.

"Hey, look at us—the early-bird club," he joked without smiling. Sara took his hand.

"I heard about your having to go," said Marsha. "That sure is crummy."

"Sure is," he said, gazing at Sara wistfully.

"Don't you think the band could play without you, though?" Marsha asked.

"Marsha!" Sara snapped. "Would you drop it? That is so tacky of you to ask him that right now."

"That's okay," said Nicky. "I don't know if they can play without me or not," he said, seeming uncomfortable with the topic. "You'll have to ask the rest of the band."

"No, we can't play without you," Sara insisted. "There's no way." She pulled him by the hand and led him away from Marsha's locker. "I'm sorry, Marsha. I really am."

"Great," Marsha muttered sarcastically. "It's nice to know you can depend on your friends."

Marsha wanted to be understanding, but she was too disappointed. She knew Sara must feel badly about Nicky, but she had been counting on them to draw votes her way. She had liked the idea of having such a cool campaign tactic. She figured that by having a rock band at her rally she'd seem like a girl who was really up on things.

Marsha went around school and checked her posters. She took down one on which someone had scribbled the words: DORIS IS THE BEST. MARSHA IS A PEST. She tried not to let her feelings be hurt by it. It was probably Doris herself who wrote it.

As it got close to homeroom time, Marsha kept her eye out for Rissa. She half hoped that she'd come by her locker. Then they could patch things up. Marsha felt it was up to Rissa to make the first move. After all, she was the one who had wrecked Marsha's hair, and *she* had said the friendship was over. Marsha even lingered by her locker a while, idly stacking her books in size order just in case Rissa showed up. But at five minutes to homeroom, there was still no sign of her. *I don't care,* Marsha said to herself angrily. *If Rissa's going to be stubborn, I can be stubborn too.*

Bobby came by and walked her to her homeroom. "If you're free next Saturday, would you feel like seeing another movie?" he asked. "Maybe we could even see the whole thing this time," he added with a mischievous grin.

"Very funny. I'd love to if you don't mind seeing whatever's at the Twin," said Marsha. Drinking in the sight of him and the very sound of his voice cheered her up.

"No problem." He laughed. "And I'll leave the bike home this time."

"That will make my parents extremely happy," she said as they reached the door of her homeroom.

"I guess I'll see you later," he said, and ran off down the hall to his own homeroom. Marsha leaned up against the doorway. She was sure now. Bobby was going to be her boyfriend. Two dates—two Saturdays in a row—would just about make it official.

As she took her seat, she noticed that Doris and Heather were deep in conversation. Marsha forced herself to ignore them and began to doodle in her notebook. *Mrs. Bobby Turner,* she wrote. No. Too old-fashioned. *Ms. Marsha Turner.* No. *Mrs. Marsha Kranton-Turner.* That might work. She'd decide whether to use Ms. or Mrs. when the time came.

After Mrs. Ritter took attendance, there was a crackle over the PA system. Every Tuesday, Theresa Rogers, the senior class president who had been elected at the end of last year, spoke, making general student announcements.

"Good morning. I have a note for sophomores.

Marty Barrow has dropped out of the election race. He says he has decided he wants to devote all his time to the Audiovisual Club. The sophomore race now consists of Marsha Kranton and Doris Gaylord—both in homeroom One-C.''

Marsha noticed Heather and Doris exchanging pleased grins. She wondered if they had had anything to do with Marty's dropping out.

''Another note for underclassmen. Our gracious principal, Mr. Handleman, has agreed to turn the PA system over to the presidential candidates between two-thirty and three o'clock tomorrow. The three freshman candidates and two sophomore candidates will each get five minutes to speak. Thursday, juniors will be able to address the school in the same time slot. Candidates don't have to speak, but those who want to, may.''

The girl went on with several more announcements, but Marsha wasn't listening. She would have to come up with something interesting to say by tomorrow. She wished they had given her at least until Thursday.

The bell for first period rang and Marsha got up from her seat. ''See you at two-thirty tomorrow,'' said Doris, gloating like a cat who'd swallowed a canary.

Marsha turned away, not wanting to speak to Doris. Then something disturbing occurred to her. ''Did you know about this?'' she asked.

''I was the one who suggested it to Mr. Handleman Friday afternoon. He thought it was a fabulous idea.'' Still smirking, Doris joined Heather at the front of the class.

Marsha met up with Sara in the hall right after class. ''I heard the announcement,'' Sara said. ''Do you know what you're going to say?''

"No," Marsha answered. "But I'll think of something."

A guilty look spread over Sara's face. "Nicky and I were going to have lunch together. I could help you write a speech during study hall, though. Nicky and I were both going to get library passes, but I'll be able to help you the second half of the period."

"Don't worry about it," said Marsha glumly. "We can work on the speech this afternoon."

"Would you mind if I didn't do it this afternoon, either?" Sara asked. "Nicky and I were going to go to the record store. I wanted to get him some tapes as a going-away present. He has to come with me to pick them out. We won't have that much more time together, so I want to make every second count. I feel terrible because I know I promised to help you. But I never expected this to happen with Nicky. You can't imagine—"

"I said, forget it," Marsha snapped. "I'll do it myself."

That evening, Marsha laid on her bed and jotted down notes for her speech. What did she really have to say? What would she do if she were elected?

Okay, Marsha, what's important to you? she asked herself. There was the library issue—being able to spend the *whole* study period in the library rather than just fifteen minutes. She knew the science lab needed new equipment. These were hardly hot issues. Maybe she should be more general and just promise to do a good job.

On Wednesday afternoon at two-twenty, Marsha was excused from her last-period honors English class to go to the principal's office. As Marsha walked to the office, she reread the speech she'd written the night before. The paper was now smudged and worn from at least five revisions. She'd done her final revision during her study period an hour ago.

She waited behind the secretary's desk while the freshmen gave their speeches through the microphone on a table in the far corner of the room.

She sat and read over her speech for what seemed like the hundredth time. It unnerved her to look at Doris, who sat two chairs down and primped in a small pocket mirror as if she were going on TV instead of onto the PA system. She seemed so confident and pleased with herself.

"Who would like to go next?" asked Mrs. Smith, the principal's secretary.

"I need a few more minutes, let her go," Doris said sweetly.

Marsha knit her brow. Doris didn't seem to be doing a thing. What did she need more time for? "I'll go, I guess," she said to Mrs. Smith.

Taking her seat in front of the microphone, Marsha began to speak. "I'm Marsha Kranton, and I believe I'll make the best choice for sophomore class president," she began, her voice shaking with nervousness. She called on all the skills she'd learned last year in debate club and breathed deeply to steady herself. "I'm running because I want the sophomores to have a strong voice in the student council. I am committed to doing the very best job possible to make sure sophomores get the attention they deserve." Marsha was pleased with the way she sounded now. She was on a roll, her voice confident and steady.

"I will represent all the students, not just a small faction." She liked that veiled dig at Doris and her in crowd. She went on to talk in general terms about her promise to give the presidency her all. "I hope you

87

will all vote for me," she concluded. "I don't think you will be disappointed."

"Very nice," said Mrs. Smith when she was done. "You can go back to class now."

"Don't I get to hear Doris's speech?" Marsha asked.

"You'll hear it in your classroom," said Mrs. Smith. "All freshman and sophomore classes are listening to the speeches."

"Run along," simpered Doris as she sashayed over to the microphone.

Marsha glared at her and left the office. Walking through the halls back to class, she felt good. Let Doris try to beat that speech. Doris's high-pitched voice would probably sound silly over the PA. She smiled at the thought.

The minute she got back to English, she realized something was wrong. The class was looking up intently at the PA box, engrossed in the announcement. But instead of hearing Doris's voice, Marsha heard her own!

"I didn't even want to be in this thing, Sara signed me up," she heard herself say. There was a whirr as the tape recorder fast-forwarded.

"You athletes might want to note this next segment," came Doris's voice, sounding very girlish.

There was a click and then Marsha's voice came on again. ". . . I'll promise to have the soccer field paved over and turned into a motorcycle racecourse."

"So much for my opponent's statement that she would help all students. She wants to do this because she's going with a boy who has a motorcycle." Marsha's classmates turned and looked at her with shocked expressions.

"I was making a . . . a . . . joke," Marsha stammered.

"Here's another anti-athlete statement," Doris continued. ". . . I'd like to see Mrs. Haggler abducted by gym-teacher–eating aliens." The class laughed at this, but Marsha cringed. When Mrs. Haggler heard about this she'd have Marsha doing squat thrusts until her legs fell off.

"And here's a statement you should hear," said Doris.

There was more fast-forwarding noise and again Marsha's voice came on. "I'm nervous about whether or not I'll be able to handle it."

There was a pause and Marsha could make out Mrs. Smith's voice in the background. "I think that's just about enough of that, Doris."

"But I have more," Doris protested in a muffled voice. It sounded like a hand was covering the microphone.

"No, you don't. If I hadn't stepped out of the room I'd have stopped you sooner," Mrs. Smith replied. By now, kids in every classroom were laughing at the private conversation that could be heard everywhere in the building.

"I don't see why," Doris began to argue. Then there was a snap and the PA went silent. Obviously Mrs. Smith had shut the system off.

Marsha slumped down in her seat. "Did you know you were being taped?" asked Ms. Morris, her English teacher, looking at her. Marsha shook her head miserably. "I didn't think so," Ms. Morris said. "Class, disregard that disgraceful display of dirty politics."

The class murmured that they would, but Marsha knew that damage had been done.

Chapter Thirteen

When she woke up on Thursday morning, Marsha was undecided as to what to do. Half of her wanted to hide under the covers. The other half wanted to get to school and punch Doris right in the nose. She'd come straight home from school the day before with a splitting headache. She'd left immediately after English, not even going back to her locker.

Sara had called and so had Bobby, but she asked her mother to say she was asleep. She was so mortified that she didn't want to talk to anyone.

No, she couldn't hide like a quitter. She had a campaign to attend to and a potential steady boyfriend to see. Marsha knew she'd have to find a way to recover from the blow Doris had dealt her.

When she got to school, she immediately realized that kids were looking at her strangely. She smiled at them, but noticed that they turned away quickly— and all because of that rotten tape. The interested buzz of excitement that had surrounded her on Monday had changed into silent stares. She fought back tears as she headed toward her locker.

As she approached her locker, she saw a small crowd of kids gathered around a sign. One boy noticed her coming toward them and said something to the others. The students looked at Marsha and quickly dispersed. Marsha was left alone to read the sign. Her blood ran cold as the meaning of the words in front of her sank in.

DON'T VOTE FOR A RAT

Gary Herman now has a month of detention Saturdays thanks to candidate Marsha Kranton. A reliable source has informed us that candidate Kranton is a spy for Mr. Ames. She regularly reports on students to the dean. Is this the kind of rat fink you want as class president? We don't think so. Vote for Doris Gaylord—a candidate who is loyal to her classmates.

Marsha's hand covered her open mouth. She was completely mortified. She looked up and down the hallway. On both sides of her, small clusters of students were watching her read the sign. She felt her face turn a hot red.

She opened her mouth to speak. At first no words came out. Then she managed to say, "It's a lie," in a voice much smaller than she had intended. "It's not true."

The students went back to what they were doing. "This is a rotten lie!" Marsha managed in a slightly stronger voice. But no one said anything.

With one swift, furious motion, Marsha ripped down the sign and tore it in half. She bit her lip to keep from crying. She knew Doris was rotten, but this was vicious even for her. How had she even found out it had been Marsha who told Mrs. Ritter about Gary?

As Marsha stood holding the two halves of the sign, Rissa came around the corner to her locker. "You saw them, huh?" she said.

91

"Them?" Marsha echoed. She realized that Rissa was holding several crumpled posters in her hands. "How many of those things did you pull down?" Marsha asked.

"You just got the eighth one," Rissa told her.

"Are there any more?"

"I don't know," Rissa answered. "Sara's up checking the second floor." Rissa picked up the two pieces of the sign which Marsha had let drop to the ground. She crumpled them with the rest and stuffed them into a metal trash container in the corner of the hall. "You still mad at me?" she asked.

"I don't know," Marsha said, leaning back, dazed, against her locker. "You're the one who's been ignoring me."

"Sorry," said Rissa. "I thought I was still mad at you until I heard Doris's speech yesterday. What a creep! Then I came in today and saw this trash. This is such a crock. Sara told me what really happened."

"The note said his father was at the hospital. I figured it was an emergency," Marsha said.

"Yeah, but unfortunately you figured wrong. Gary's father was at the hospital because he's a doctor. He wanted to talk to Gary because Mr. Ames had just called to tell him that Gary had cut school last week."

"Oooohhh," Marsha moaned. She turned and pressed her forehead against her locker. "Stupid! Stupid! Stupid!" she berated herself.

"Stop that," chided Rissa, grabbing Marsha's arm. "Banging your head against a locker doesn't look very presidential. You didn't know. I told Doris it was an innocent mistake."

Marsha was confused. "You talked to Doris about this?"

A sheepish look came over Rissa's face. "Yeah.

Yesterday, just before your speech. I heard her talking about some little creep who had turned Gary in. I just assumed she somehow knew it was you. So I said to her, 'Marsha didn't mean to get Gary into trouble.' "

Marsha nodded slowly, getting the picture. "But she didn't know it was me, did she?"

Rissa winced and shook her head.

"But now she knows—because you told her," Marsha concluded in a voice which was eerily calm.

"Yes, but it was a misunderstanding—just like what you did was a mis—"

"Rissa!" Marsha shouted angrily. "This is all your fault! You did this to me!"

"I didn't mean to!" Rissa said, defensively.

"Just like you didn't mean to wreck my hair?" Marsha cried.

"They were both mistakes. I really am sorry!" Rissa said pleadingly.

"Real friends don't make so many mistakes when it comes to their friends' feelings," yelled Marsha.

"All right, be that way!" Rissa yelled back. "For all I know, maybe you did tell on Gary because you're a snitch. Maybe I don't know you the way I thought I did!"

"That's so mean! I hate you, Rissa!" shouted Marsha, tears filling her eyes.

Rissa stepped back as if Marsha had slapped her in the face. Without saying another word, she turned and walked away. Marsha stood at her locker, breathing heavily with anger.

Rissa—of all people—had done this to her. The second bell for homeroom rang. The stream of kids heading for class began to fill the hall. Marsha felt as if they were all staring at her accusingly.

Suddenly she saw Bobby heading down the hall toward her. How could she face him? She couldn't face anyone! She might have recovered from yesterday, but this was too much! Marsha wanted to run away and disappear.

He was coming closer. She couldn't bear to see Bobby looking at her with . . . what? Shock, disappointment, contempt? She could try to tell him the truth, but would he believe her? After all, it was partly true. She had told on Gary. He would never want to be seen with a girl the whole school hated.

Bobby had told her not to campaign. He'd been right. If she'd only listened to him none of this would have happened.

Blinded with tears, with her head pounding, Marsha ran down the hall away from Bobby. She continued into the main hall and out the front doors.

Chapter Fourteen

Thursday at lunch, Rissa went to a meeting for the Girls' Sports Club. It was a new club and the lunchtime meetings were for the purpose of setting things up. Rissa liked the idea that it would deal only with sports events for girls.

Rissa leaned back in her metal folding chair and listened to Ms. Moss, the gym teacher who moderated the club meetings. But her thoughts drifted to Marsha. The truth was, she felt terrible about what had happened. Here she was supposedly Marsha's campaign manager, and she'd messed up everything. When would she ever learn to keep her mouth shut—especially around Doris?

Marsha's words, "I hate you!" echoed in her head. How could she have said that? No matter what happened, Rissa would never have told Marsha she hated her. With a small shiver, Rissa wondered if it were true.

Rissa didn't find out that Marsha had left school until she met up with Sara at the end of the day. "You guys should make up," Sara said as they walked home together. "Marsha really needs you now."

"No, she doesn't," said Rissa. "She told me she hated me."

"She said that?" Sara gasped.

Rissa nodded. Telling Sara about the fight only reinforced her bruised feelings.

"I'm sure she didn't mean it," said Sara. "I'd be pretty upset too, if someone had put up signs saying I was a stool pigeon for Mr. Ames."

"We all have problems," said Rissa icily. "My father is marrying someone I don't like that much. And I'm going to have her as my mother!"

"I thought you liked Mary," said Sara.

"I tried to like her for my father's sake, and I don't think she's the worst person in the world, but I definitely don't want her for my mother."

"She seems nice to me," said Sara, stopping to tie her sneaker.

"The problem is, it's as if she's from ancient Italy or something. She acts like she and I are the ones who should clear the table after dinner . . . like my father and the boys are too good to do these 'womanly' chores. I've never even seen her in pants. She says she hates baseball. She's always sewing a button on somebody's shirt or ironing something for one of my brothers. And she doesn't even *live* with us yet."

"That could be kind of annoying," Sara conceded.

"No kidding!" said Rissa. "If she thinks she can make me into a servant that will wait on my brothers, hand and foot, she can guess again!"

"I guess you have to make it clear how you feel," said Sara.

"You bet I will," said Rissa emphatically. She was about to turn down Fordham Street, when something occurred to her. "How are you doing? It must be rough on you, knowing that Nicky will be leaving soon."

"I don't feel like talking about it," Sara replied, looking away.

"You sure?" Rissa asked.

Sara nodded and forced a smile onto her lips. She flipped the headphones of her Walkman up from her neck and over her ears. "Hey, you were right. Everyone's got their own problems," she said, shouting slightly over the music in her ears.

It wasn't that Rissa didn't care, but she had enough to think about. She was relieved that Sara seemed to be handling Nicky's departure reasonably well. Rissa didn't know how much help she could really be to Sara. She was much too preoccupied with her father's marriage to help anyone else.

When Rissa reached home, the house was filled with the delicious aroma of something cooking. This was very strange. The sound of the microwave beeping as it finished cooking up some frozen food was usually the only indication that anyone ate at all in the Lupinski household—the beep, and the pile of frozen- and junk-food cartons they took out every night in the trash.

Rissa came into the kitchen and found Mary sprinkling dried basil over a pot of tomato sauce. "Just in time." She smiled at Rissa. "I could use some help putting this lasagna together."

Mary took a pot of boiling water and lasagna noodles off the stove and dumped them into a colander in the sink. "I left work early to surprise your father. He's been bothering me to make him lasagna for three weeks now."

Rissa noticed that Mary wore a ruffled yellow apron over her white blouse and brown tweed skirt. She was a thin woman and moved quickly and efficiently, not wasting a single motion.

"How did you get in?" Rissa asked. She had

intended to sound casual but the edge of annoyance in her voice came through.

Mary turned off the faucet. There was a helpless expression in her eyes. "Your father gave me a key the other night."

"Oh," said Rissa. She opened the refrigerator and stared inside. She wasn't hungry but she wanted to hide her angry expression from Mary. How dare she walk right into her house and start cooking! And then expect Rissa to help her out! There was no way Rissa was going to come home and start cooking lasagna after school. Why didn't she ask one of the boys?

She remembered Sara saying that Rissa would have to make her position clear. It sounded like good advice. "Look, Mary," she said. "I think you should know that I don't intend to turn into some slave class of a person just because you and my father are getting married."

Mary looked stunned. "What makes you think that will happen?" she asked.

"Look at this! You want me to start cooking already."

"I like to cook. I thought you might enjoy it," said Mary, sounding hurt.

"Well, I don't like it," Rissa said firmly.

"All right," said Mary. She took a hunk of mozzarella cheese from a plastic bag and began slicing it on a chopping board. Rissa was about to leave when Mary began to speak again. "I called my friend Father Benzoni today. He said he could marry us at Saint Ann's chapel on Saturday the thirtieth."

"Are you having a party afterwards?" Rissa asked.

"I thought we might have some people back to the house here. Of course I'll have to put up curtains and

98

have the rug cleaned. Maybe you and I can go together to have our hair done and—"

"I don't want to have my hair done," Rissa insisted.

Rissa didn't understand herself. Why was she being so ornery? Mary was only talking about fixing up the house—something Rissa herself had wanted to do. She couldn't help it. Mary seemed to bring out the worst in her.

"Of course, your being a model and all, I suppose you can do your hair yourself. Maybe you could do mine for me."

"You don't get it, do you?" Rissa raised her voice in frustration. "Yes, I'm a model, and yes, I'm a girl, but that doesn't mean I want to do all these dumb girl things with *you*." The angry words flew straight out of Rissa's mouth. The minute she'd spoken them, though, she wished she hadn't. Mary looked so hurt.

"I'm sorry, dear," Mary said. "I only thought that since your mother is gone, maybe I could make up for some of the things you've missed with—"

"I haven't missed anything!" Rissa cried. The nerve of Mary to think she could fill some kind of gap in Rissa's life. Rissa was suddenly more furious than ever.

"Rissa, I only want us to be a family."

"I already have a family, and you're not my mother," Rissa yelled. She turned to run from the kitchen and bumped straight into her father.

"You apologize to Mary right now!" he boomed.

"I won't," Rissa defied him. "I've just said what I feel."

Mr. Lupinski's face reddened with anger. "Clarissa, you apologize or you are grounded!"

"No, Pete, please," Mary interrupted. "Rissa is just upset because this is all so new and sudden. We'll get used to each other and become friends."

"Clarissa, apologize to Mary," Mr. Lupinski insisted.

Rissa faced Mary. She was a stranger who was going to start running their lives and changing everything. Look at the way her father was acting! He was already taking Mary's side against her.

Suddenly Rissa knew why she really resented Mary so much. She was going to take from Rissa what little time and attention her father had for her. Her father wasn't the warmest man in the world, but he showed his love by coming to her sports events and talking to her about sports. Now Mary would always be there. And Mary hated sports. Now that there was a woman in the house, her father might not talk to her at all. He'd always refer her to Mary.

She didn't want to talk to Mary. She wanted her father.

"Clarissa, I insist that you apologize," her father pressed. Rissa was speechless. She couldn't do it. She half wanted to, but the words wouldn't come to her lips.

"We don't want anyone at our wedding who doesn't wish us well," her father stated.

"Fine, then I won't come," Rissa said defiantly.

"If that's how you feel, then it's fine with me, too," he replied.

"Pete, no!" cried Mary. "You don't mean that." But Mr. Lupinski ignored her.

"I'm serious, Clarissa," he said.

"So am I," Rissa exploded. She fled up the stairs into her room. She threw herself face-down on her bed and sobbed uncontrollably. She'd been right about Mary all along, Rissa thought, heartbroken. Her father would always put Mary first from now on.

Chapter Fifteen

Marsha sat up in bed on Friday morning. Driving rain pounded against the windowpane and thunder boomed in the distance. She'd come home Thursday morning and gone straight back to bed. Her parents had already left for work, and when they came home she said she felt sick. It had been partly true. She felt sick with humiliation, anger, and disappointment.

Marsha needed to think. She wondered if her parents could have her transferred to the Elmsly district school. Her aunt lived in Elmsly and she could use her address. It was a shame, because she was just starting to feel comfortable at Rosemont High. But she could never go back—not when she'd been branded as the school snitch.

Elmsly was awfully close, though. Marsha wondered if kids would hear about her and shun her before they even got to know her. Probably.

She'd read about girls who went to boarding schools in Europe. She should probably go to Spain, since she was studying Spanish in school. She'd only heard of boarding schools in Switzerland or France, but there had to be others.

Marsha decided to write to Lena, the Swiss foreign exchange student who'd stayed with Sara last summer. Lena might know about European schools. Maybe she could even live with Lena if her parents objected to paying for a boarding school.

Marsha got out of bed and went to her desk to look for a piece of stationery. She rarely wrote to anyone but she knew she had a box of stationery somewhere in her desk. She dug through old diaries and keepsakes until she found a squashed box of blue rainbow-bordered paper at the bottom of the drawer. As she took the box from the drawer, a green book caught her eye. It was her fifth-grade graduation book from Rosemont Elementary.

She took it out and sat back down on her bed. She opened the book to the middle where she knew her class portrait was. She and Sara were sitting in the front rows with the short kids. Rissa was in the back line with the tall kids. All three smiled at the camera with bright eyes.

They looked so much younger than they did now. The Makeover Club had really made a difference. Marsha could see now why bratty Johnny Keane used to call her Marsha-mallow. She was so short and pudgy. Her straight brown hair was cut in a round bowl style and her rimless glasses made her look like an owl.

Sara looked very different, too. Marsha had almost forgotten what her real hair color looked like. It was a mousy shade of brownish-blonde which hung limply to her shoulders. Sara's smile was a silver mine of braces and her skinny elbows jutted out from a flowered short-sleeve blouse.

Next, Marsha studied Rissa. Even in fifth grade she was tall and stocky. Her short hair stuck up in a cowlick at the back of her head. All the other kids were dressed in their best clothes, but Rissa had on a polo shirt and jeans. Marsha remembered that Rissa had claimed to not remember it was picture day. Now it occurred to Marsha that Rissa probably hadn't even owned a dress back then.

As Marsha continued to look at the picture, her mother stuck her head in the door. "How are you feeling this morning? Any better?"

"Ummm . . . sick. Still sick," Marsha lied.

Her mother sat beside her on the bed and looked at the book. "You girls sure go back a long way together," she commented. "You were all so adorable. Look at Rissa! She sure has changed. You all have."

Marsha nodded sadly. "We were such good friends," she said ruefully.

"What do you mean *were*?" asked Mrs. Kranton.

"They've really let me down in this campaign," said Marsha. "Sara promised that her band would play for me and then she backed out. And Rissa . . . Rissa did the worst thing . . ." Marsha's eyes filled with tears. She looked away from her mother.

"What is it, honey?" her mother asked.

Losing all control, Marsha told her everything that had gone on in the past few days, starting with the horrible phone call incident and Doris's taped announcement. She went on to tell her about snitching on Gary and then reading about it on the posters. And finally, between sobs, she told her mother about how Rissa had been the one to tell Doris. "I really feel okay today," she admitted, "but I can't go back to that school—ever again."

Mrs. Kranton rubbed her chin pensively. "I'm really sorry about what happened to you, but I think you're being too hard on Sara and Rissa," she said.

"I'm not. Besides, it doesn't matter now. I want to talk to you about something." Marsha paused, trying to find the best way to put her next statement.

"I want to go to school in Europe. I know it's expensive, but once I'm there I could get a job. Maybe I could teach English and—"

"Hold on, hold on," her mother said, trying to hold back a light laugh. "I don't think you have to go to another continent because someone told a lie about you."

"You don't understand!" cried Marsha. "I knew you wouldn't. Everyone in the school hates me now!"

"I'm sure that's not true," said her mother.

"Oh, it's true. You should have seen the way they were looking at me," Marsha insisted.

"They were probably just curious to see how you would react," Mrs. Kranton suggested. "How did you react?"

"I came home," Marsha admitted.

Mrs. Kranton sighed. "Didn't that make you seem guilty?"

"I don't know . . . maybe. I *am* guilty, though."

"You're not," said her mother. "You did what you thought was best for the boy, under the circumstances. You believed you were acting in his best interest."

"I know, but—"

"So, tell the kids that," said her mother. "Don't wimp out. Doris isn't the only one who can put up signs."

"I guess I could put up signs giving my side of the story," said Marsha, following her mother's thinking.

"That's right. Stand up and fight."

"Do you think anyone would believe it?" asked Marsha.

"You won't know until you try," said her mother, getting up off the bed.

"Mom, there's another thing. I've been avoiding

Bobby because I figure he must think I'm the worst person in the world."

"Are you the worst person in the world?" asked her mother.

"Of course not!" cried Marsha, shocked that her mother would ask such a thing.

"That's right. You're one of the best people I know," said her mother. "Bobby must know that too."

"But he doesn't really know me that well," Marsha pointed out.

"Would you give him the benefit of the doubt if the situation were reversed?" asked Mrs. Kranton.

"Sure," said Marsha. She saw what her mother was getting at. "All right. I'll go and explain things to him. I guess I owe him that much."

"That's my girl," said Mrs. Kranton.

"Could I stay home this morning and make up the signs?" Marsha asked.

"All right," said her mother, heading out the door.

Marsha sat down at her desk and opened her loose-leaf binder. *I, Marsha Kranton, want to tell the real story of the Gary Herman case*, she wrote. She began framing what she would say. She knew it had to be as brief and honest as possible. Soon, it began to flow easily. She wrote:

Ask Gary and he'll tell you that his father is a doctor. Brilliant me, I assumed his father was in the hospital because he was hurt or ill. I thought Gary needed to receive his father's message, she finished up. *But obviously I thought wrong.* She read over what she'd written, and then added, *It was a dumb mistake, but ask yourself what you would have done in my position.*

She leaned back in her chair. She had a lot to do. First she had to buy the materials for the signs. Then she had to write them out and hang them up.

Marsha went to her mirror and looked into her eyes. Did she have what it took to be a leader? Or would she fold up when things got rough? She reached into her top drawer and pulled out her spare pair of glasses. She hadn't worn them in a long while.

She put them on and looked in the mirror. They did make her look more serious. *Okay*, she thought, *if my classmates need someone to look the part of a serious student, then I'll do it*.

She took a plastic tortoiseshell headband from the top of her dresser and pushed her bangs back. She'd never land on the cover of *Seventeen* with this look, but that wasn't what she was after. She had to win this election now. It was no longer a lark or a bid to boost her status in school. Her very reputation was at stake. And she was going to do whatever it took to win!

Chapter Sixteen

Sara bent her head against the pouring rain and tried to keep her umbrella from snapping back in the wind. "Darn," she grumbled as she stepped off the curb into a puddle, soaking her black high-top sneakers. Kids streamed past her, their colorful umbrellas buffeted in the wind. They headed through the chainlink gate at the back of school. She didn't even bother to look for Rissa and Marsha. Marsha was probably already there, campaigning. And Rissa almost always overslept on rainy days.

A yellow school bus turned the corner and splashed her purple, hooded slicker with muddy water. "Thanks a lot!" she called after it. Several more buses drove into the parking lot of Rosemont High.

She was about to follow the buses in when she heard someone calling her name. She turned and saw Nicky, drenched to the skin, running up behind her.

"Are you crazy?" she asked, holding her umbrella over his head. "You're soaked."

"I couldn't find an umbrella," he said. "I had to see you. My dad got a call last night. There's some big corporate takeover happening that they didn't expect so soon. Anyway, it means they want him in Hong Kong the day after tomorrow, so we're leaving tonight."

"It wasn't supposed to be until next week," Sara protested.

"I know, but they need him to protect the companies' interests during the merger. Hearing my father talk about it makes it sound like a really big deal."

"You can't go just like that," Sara pleaded.

"I know—it's too sudden," he said, putting his arm around her shoulder. "Can you skip first period this morning? Let's go to the diner for breakfast. I doubt anyone from school will come in."

Sara mentally ran down her list of classes. She had no tests. She could probably do it this once. "Okay," she said. "Let's go."

They changed direction, walking away from the school. They kept their heads down, not looking at the kids who were going toward the school. Sara noticed Mrs. Gaylord's green Jaguar stopped at a stop sign. Doris was in the passenger seat. She rolled down the window and called to Sara, "Cutting out, Marshall? Aren't you afraid your pal will turn you in?"

"Stuff it, Doris!" Sara yelled back. Doris rolled up her window abruptly as her mother pulled away from the stop.

Nicky and Sara walked into the diner, both shivering from the wet, cold weather. They took a booth and a waitress took their breakfast orders. Soon she came back with a coffee for Nicky and a hot chocolate for Sara. "Here are some paper towels to dry off with," she said, putting the roll on their table.

"Thanks," said Sara, ruffling her wet hair with a wad of paper towels. "This *can't* be happening," she said to Nicky. "I can't believe it."

"Here's the plan," said Nicky. "We'll write to each other every day. And if I don't get the job at

Hemway, I'll find another job around here for the summer. It won't be too long until I come back."

Sara forced herself to ask the question that had been on her mind for days. "Will you be seeing other girls while you're away?"

Nicky looked down at the table. "Maybe we should. It doesn't seem fair to ask you not to."

"Do *you* want to?" she asked gently.

Nicky shook his head. "No, I don't. Do you?"

"Me neither," Sara answered. "I could never feel the same about anyone else as I do about you."

"Me neither," said Nicky.

Sara's heart soared with joy and relief. Nicky never really talked much about his feelings. But this meant he loved her as much as she loved him. "You're right. It won't be so long."

Suddenly, Nicky's eyes went wide with alarm. "Duck!" he said, sliding down in his seat.

Sara, following his order, slid down. "What are we hiding from?" she asked, whispering to him under the table.

"Ames," said Nicky. "He's making a raid of the diner. Probably looking for cutters. I could care less, but I don't want you to get detention."

At that moment, the waitress arrived with their eggs. "Anything the matter?" she asked, looking down at them.

"Ummm . . . no, we're fine," Sara whispered. "We're, uh, just resting."

The waitress looked up the aisle. "It couldn't be that fat guy with the toupé who made you so tired all of a sudden, could it?" she asked, knowingly.

"As a matter of fact, yes," said Nicky, sinking lower in his seat. "He's not coming this way, is he?"

"As a matter of fact, he is," the waitress answered, putting the dishes on the table. She took out her pad and finished up their check. "Make sure you pay this tab before you're dragged out of here," she said, slipping it next to Nicky's coffee cup.

Nicky dug a ten-dollar bill from his pocket and laid it on the table. "Keep the change," he whispered.

"Thanks, kid. That just bought you a three-minute delay. I'll ask the guy if I can help him," she said.

The waitress left and Sara heard her saying, "Can I get you some breakfast this morning, sir?"

"This is so embarrassing," Sara whispered to Nicky. "I might as well turn myself in."

"No, come on," said Nicky, slipping down under the table. She slid down beside him. The two of them sat on the floor with their knees to their chins.

Sara clamped her hand over her mouth as Mr. Ames's gray trousers appeared right outside their booth. Suddenly her chest heaved with a nervous hiccup. She looked to Nicky with panicked eyes.

He puffed his cheeks, signaling her to hold her breath. Sara tried, but another muffled hiccup escaped her lips. She covered her mouth with both hands, and Nicky put his hand over hers.

She looked into his eyes and saw that they were lit up with laughter. She had to turn away so he didn't make her laugh, as well. If Mr. Ames caught her, it would be no laughing matter.

Apparently Mr. Ames had seen them, or *something* had caught his attention. His shiny black shoes turned to the front and then the back of the restaurant. He checked the booths on either side of theirs. "Miss," he called to the waitress, "were two kids sitting here? I see breakfasts but no customers."

"I don't know. The other waitress has that table—she's in the kitchen now," the waitress lied.

Mr. Ames turned around again. Luckily, it hadn't occurred to him to look down.

Sara's frame shook with another quiet hiccup. "Little monsters must have sneaked past me," she heard Mr. Ames mutter before he walked away.

Nicky took his hand from Sara's mouth. "That was close," he whispered, looking into her eyes.

"Very close," she agreed.

The next thing Sara knew, they were kissing, there under the table. Sara held Nicky tight and wished the moment would last forever. She felt like a heroine in a movie who had been saved from the bad guys by her hero. She never would have thought that the most romantic moment in her life would take place under a table in a diner. But there they were—and it felt wonderful.

A sharp rap on the table made Sara jump and almost bump her head. "The coast is clear," the waitress told them.

They came out from their hiding place. "Thanks very much," Nicky said to the waitress.

"I'm not doing that again," she replied. "We could get into a lot of trouble with the school. From now on I'm not serving any kids until after school hours."

"You won't see us again before three," Sara assured her.

"I'd better not," the waitress warned. "I let it go this time 'cause you kids seem like you're into something important."

"We are," said Sara. "We're not going to see each other again for a long time."

"Okay then, well, okay," said the waitress. "Just eat up and get out of here."

Their breakfast was already getting cold, and Sara found she didn't have much of an appetite anyway. Nicky just picked at his eggs. They sat holding hands across the table as the rain pelted against the windowpane beside them. They felt sad, but it felt good to be sad together.

"I'd better get home and pack," said Nicky after a while. "We have to catch a four o'clock flight. Could you go down to the office and tell them that . . . I won't be back? If it's too much of a hassle, don't do it. I'll have to call them, anyway, once I have my new school's address, so they can send my records."

At his last statement, Sara blinked away more tears. "I'll do it," she managed to answer.

They left the diner, and Nicky walked Sara back toward the school. They stopped a block away. "You're between classes now. If you hurry, you can slip into your next class. Then you'll be marked late instead of absent," he said.

Sara threw her arms around him, letting her open umbrella fall to the ground. "Nicky, I love you so much," she said passionately.

"And I love you too, Sara," he said, stroking her wet hair. "You don't know how much I'll miss you."

He kissed her forehead and then stooped to pick up her umbrella. "Better go," he said, putting it in her hand. He kissed her once more on the lips and then placed his hands on her shoulders and turned her toward the school. "Just walk, and don't turn around. I'll start my letter on the plane," he whispered in her ear.

She squeezed his hand and began to walk. She didn't want to cry, but immediately two tears rolled down her cheeks. She walked half a block, letting her tears mix with the rain on her face. Then she couldn't take it anymore. She turned around to see him.

But he was gone.

Sara stared at the empty space where he had stood. Then she wiped her eyes and headed into school. She walked in through the back door, trying to hide the fact that she'd just arrived, and closed her umbrella.

As Nicky had said, she was in luck. Classes were changing and the halls were filled with students. Leaving a trail of water behind her, she made her way to her locker. As she stashed her wet gear inside the locker, and grabbed her second-period math book, Sara made a mental note to get down to the office later and tell them Nicky wouldn't be coming back.

Sara had to pass Marsha's locker on her way to math. She was surprised to see Marsha there, pulling off a wet, tan raincoat. Sara realized Marsha herself was just getting in.

Sara wondered why Marsha was late, but she was glad to see her. She really needed a friend today. She wanted to smooth over the bad feelings between them, and tell Marsha how badly she felt about the hand not playing.

Marsha sensed her approach and looked up at Sara.

"Oh my gosh!" Sara gasped. "What happened to you?"

Chapter Seventeen

"I'm going all-out to win this election, Sara," said Marsha tartly.

"Wow! You're not kidding around, are you? You look so . . . different."

"You and Rissa told me I needed a clean-cut image, so here it is," said Marsha, shutting her locker with a crisp click. She tucked the short ends of her hair behind her headband and adjusted her glasses. She wore a blue tailored shirt and a neatly pleated gray skirt. She had on a pair of polished loafers and light gray stockings. Her only frills were a light coat of pink lipstick and a pair of small button earrings.

"You sure do look serious," Sara had to admit.

"The next three years of my school life here at Rosemont depend on my winning," said Marsha, heading down the hall. "When this election is over, I'll either be class president or an outcast."

"Don't you think you're exaggerating just a little?" asked Sara, hurrying along after her.

"What do you care?" said Marsha. "You're too busy to have the band play at my rally. You only cared about doing it because Nicky would be there. It wasn't important enough to do it without him."

Sara grabbed Marsha by the sleeve. "Stop it! Stop being so selfish and self-centered!"

Marsha was stunned. How could Sara say *she* was being selfish? "I'm not the one who broke a promise."

"You don't even care that Nicky is leaving. You don't care how it's making me feel." Sara spoke angrily.

"You seemed all right about it. You didn't make it seem like such a big deal," Marsha defended herself.

"You should have known it was a big deal!" Sara shouted. "Friends are supposed to know these things. Do I have to tell you everything?"

"I'm not a mind reader," said Marsha.

"And you're not much of a friend either!" yelled Sara. "You have Bobby and you're running for class president—but look at me! I lost Nicky and I'll probably lose the band!"

Marsha and Sara glared at each other angrily. Just as Marsha was about to throw an answer back at her, the bell for class sounded. They spied Rissa rushing down the hall. Her hair was still wet and she looked as if she'd just come in from outside. Neither Marsha nor Sara was surprised. Rissa always overslept on rainy days.

Rissa stopped short when she saw Sara and Marsha. "What's going on?" she asked.

"I'm mad at you too!" Sara attacked her.

"Me?" Rissa gasped, taken by surprise. "What did I do to you?"

"It's what you didn't do. Friends are supposed to care about each other."

"I asked how you were feeling the other day!" Rissa exclaimed.

"But I could tell you were just being polite. You didn't really want to know."

Rissa didn't argue. She knew Sara was right.

"And now Nicky's gone!" said Sara, bursting into

tears once again. "He and his father leave tonight for Hong Kong."

Marsha put her arm around Sara. "You must feel terrible."

Sara covered her eyes with one hand and nodded. "I feel like there's a big empty hole inside of me."

"You still have us," said Marsha tenderly.

"It doesn't feel like I do," Sara cried in a tear-choked voice.

Marsha and Rissa exchanged guilty glances. "I've been so upset about my father getting married, I haven't been much of a friend," said Rissa, her eyes filling with tears. "Do you know I'm not even going to the wedding?"

"Why?" Sara asked, horrified.

"My father wants me to apologize to Mary about something, when all I was doing was being honest with her about my feelings. I'm not going to do that."

"Maybe you should," said Marsha.

Rissa shook her head. "But that doesn't give me an excuse to forget about both of your problems. I'm really sorry."

"Me too," said Marsha. She felt her eyes mist up. "I've been kind of crummy to both of you, too."

Sara looked at them with red-rimmed eyes. "Why are you both crying?"

"Because I can't stand to see you cry," said Marsha, dashing away a tear with her hand.

"Me neither," said Rissa.

"I should have talked to you both more," Sara admitted. "I guess you can't tell how I feel unless I tell you."

Marsha saw exactly what had happened. She and Rissa had been so wrapped up in their own problems that they hadn't bothered about Sara, or about each other. And Sara hadn't trusted them enough to insist on their help.

"Boy, look at us, standing here crying in the middle of the hall," said Rissa. "What a sorry sight we must be."

At the same time, the three girls looked around at the empty hall.

"Well, nobody better see us, or we're in trouble. We're going to get cut slips if we don't move," said Sara, heading for the girls' restroom. "Looks like I'm missing math."

"Skipping class isn't too presidential, but I guess I've got no choice," said Marsha, following Sara and Rissa into the restroom.

"I did the same unfair thing to you that you did to me," Marsha said to Rissa. "You made an honest mistake. I guess I was looking for someone to blame. I'm sorry."

"Me too," Rissa said, hugging her. Marsha hugged her back. Sara put her arms around both of them. Marsha smiled for the first time in days. It felt good to be friends again.

Sara splashed cold water on her face and dried it with a paper towel. "I lost my boyfriend today, but at least I got my friends back."

"It stinks that he had to go," said Rissa.

"And all I could think about was my rally," Marsha said, blaming herself.

"I don't think the band can manage without Nicky," Sara told her sadly.

"It's okay," said Marsha. "I know you would do it if you could. I was just disappointed."

Since they were stuck in the restroom until the next bell, Marsha told them about her plan to defend herself. "I have all these posters in my locker. I'm going to put them up at lunchtime."

Sara then told them about her close brush with Mr. Ames—and about kissing Nicky under the table.

"That's so romantic," said Marsha.

"Wasn't it a little cramped?" asked Rissa.

"No, it was wonderful." Sara sighed.

Before they knew it, the next bell had rung and they had to hurry to class. All through math, Marsha was conscious of her classmates stealing sidelong glances at her as though she were some sort of oddity. Marsha wondered if they were noticing her new, serious, presidential look. Or maybe they were thinking, *What a creep!*

Next period was science lab. Marsha's heart pounded as she approached the classroom. She knew Bobby would be there. She hadn't seen him since Doris's sign went up yesterday. He hadn't called her at home, either.

She stopped and hesitated at the door, then took off her glasses and opened the top button of her shirt. She couldn't bring herself to face Bobby with such a prissy appearance. She prayed that he'd smile, and seem happy to see her.

Bobby was already seated at the lab table. He looked up when she came in, but he didn't smile. Marsha saw his eyes shift uneasily. She took a deep breath and resolved to explain the whole thing to him.

"Bobby—"

"Marsha—" he said at the same time.

"You go first," she told him.

"Okay," he said. "I want to know why you ran away when you saw me coming yesterday. If you don't want to go out with me, say so. But don't play these dumb games with me."

"No, it wasn't that," said Marsha. "You saw that sign yesterday about me telling on a kid. I was just so embarrassed."

"Maybe you should be embarrassed," he said.

Marsha was shocked. "What do you mean? It was a lie."

"Maybe you should be embarrassed that you're even running in this thing, I mean," he stated. "Ever since you began the campaign, Doris has put you into one idiotic position after the other. What are you trying to prove? That you're as popular as she is?"

"You are ashamed to be seen with me, aren't you?" Marsha said. "That's what this is really all about, isn't it."

"I told you this whole president thing was dumb," he said.

"Don't avoid the question," she insisted. "Are you embarrassed to be seen with me?"

"No," he said.

Marsha was unconvinced. "I think you are. Maybe we'd better not go to the movies this Saturday if that's how you feel."

"I didn't say that—"

"It's all right," she cut him off. Marsha didn't believe him. He didn't want to be seen with her. "Believe me, it's fine with me," she said icily.

"I just want you to think about what you're doing," he said.

"I really couldn't care less," said Marsha, covering her wounded feelings. "I was going to cancel it anyway."

"You were?" he asked.

"Yes. I didn't think we had that much in common, to be honest with you," she said.

"Okay," he replied sullenly. "You're right. Maybe we do see things very differently."

Well, thought Marsha. *That was easy enough. He didn't even argue.* They sat beside one another, only speaking when they had to confer on the slides they were looking at under the microscope. Marsha couldn't see a thing without her glasses, so she put them back on.

"I never knew you wore glasses," he commented.

"Now you know," she answered flatly.

"You look very different today," he said.

"It's the new me," she replied with a cold laugh. The minute biology was over, Marsha rushed from the room, angry and upset. Now Doris's smear campaign had cost her a boyfriend. He didn't want to be seen with her. She was sure of it.

I'll get you back, Doris! she thought. *This is really war now!*

She grabbed her posters from her locker and headed down to the cafeteria to meet Sara and Rissa. Her growling stomach convinced her to go grab a sandwich while she waited for them.

In order to get to the food line, Marsha would have to pass the table where Doris and her friends were sitting. As Marsha neared them, Doris swiveled around in her seat and smiled nastily at her. Marsha saw her whisper something to Heather that caused the girl to smirk.

Marsha tried not to look at them, but as she approached, she heard a low booing sound. Within seconds, hisses started coming from the table in front of Doris. Marsha held her head up high and continued to look straight ahead, her heart beating wildly.

The booing and hissing got louder as a third table joined in, and then a fourth. Someone shot a straw wrapper at her shoulder. Marsha felt as though she could hardly breathe. An embarrassed blush was forming at her temples. She desperately wanted to run away.

Instead, she turned around and faced the booing crowd of students. There was no way she'd let them get the best of her today.

Chapter Eighteen

Rissa walked into the cafeteria and was stunned to see Marsha standing and facing tables of booing and hissing students. By now, kids at every table had their eyes on Marsha, fascinated by the scene.

"Hurry up," she called to Sara, who was still out in the hall. The two of them walked quickly into the cafeteria and headed toward Marsha.

"You'll get the real story if you look at the posters I'm about to put up," Marsha was telling them. "My opponent is conducting a malicious smear campaign and I want you all to know it."

"Nice try, Kranton," yelled Doris. "But don't try to worm out of it. Everyone knows you're Ames's spy."

"That's a lie," Marsha spoke up, concentrating on keeping the quiver of nervousness from her voice.

"And we all know what a good liar you are, Doris!" Rissa said, coming up beside Marsha.

Sara held up a stack of white paper. "I have leaflets here, telling the whole story," she announced. She and Rissa had had a study hall together and had written up Marsha's story. The wording was different from the posters, but the message was the same. They'd then gotten library passes and spent five dollars running off two hundred and fifty copies.

Marsha took a leaflet from the top of the pile and scanned it quickly. MARSHA KRANTON—A CANDIDATE WHO'S NOT AFRAID, read the headline. It went on to say Marsha would be willing to do what she thought was right, no matter what the consequence.

Rissa began handing out the papers. The first ones went to tables with the angriest groups of kids. Sara passed them out to the other tables. "Come on, guys," she said when she got to Stingo, Eric, and Sam's table. She handed them each a stack of papers. "Start giving them out." Without arguing, the boys helped distribute the leaflets.

Rissa noticed Mike and her brother Roger coming toward her. "Give us some of those," said Roger, taking a stack from Rissa. He took a pile and gave half of it to Mike.

Rissa smiled at them. "Varsity basketball supports candidate Kranton," Mike announced. As team captain, he took it upon himself to speak for the entire basketball team.

"That's right, Marsha Kranton is pro-sports," Rissa cried, still handing out fliers. "Come hear her speak tomorrow at an open meeting of the Girls' Sports Club."

Marsha's jaw dropped in surprise, but she rose to the occasion. "I'll discuss all my issues there and at any club that will invite me to speak," she shouted above the growing din of students who were talking about her fliers.

Rissa turned and noticed Sara standing on a folding chair. "And be sure to come to our rally on election day, September thirtieth!" Sara announced. "The Eggheads will be performing at Marsha's area."

Rissa exchanged glances with Marsha. They looked at the band members, who had stopped handing out leaflets. Eric, Stingo, and Sam were all staring at Sara in surprise.

"It's going to be a great show! Isn't it, guys?" Sara said confidently to the other band members.

Eric and Sam looked at Stingo who had always been second in command after Nicky. He shrugged his shoulders and then smiled. "A great show, don't miss it!" he said, smiling.

Doris had jumped up. "This girl is a liar!" she shouted, pointing at Marsha. She pulled Gary Herman to his feet. "Tell them what happened, Gary!"

The cafeteria quieted down. Gary looked around uncomfortably. All eyes were on him. "Didn't she turn you in?" Doris demanded loudly.

Gary nodded. "But isn't your father a doctor?" Marsha countered. "And didn't he send a message for you to call him at the hospital?"

"Yeah," he agreed reluctantly.

"Gary!" Doris shrieked.

"Sorry, Doris," he said. "A person might make that mistake."

"You heard it here!" Rissa boomed. "A person might make that mistake says Gary Herman himself!"

A group of pro-Doris students gathered on the other side of the cafeteria and began chanting, "Dor-is! Dor-is!" Doris left her seat and joined the chanters. She stood on a chair smiling and waving to the cheerers.

Suddenly, a shrill whistle cut through the noise. It was Mr. Ames. "Everybody off the chairs, and keep the noise to a dull roar."

Rissa saw her chance and grabbed it. "Mr. Ames," she shouted from across the room. "Has Marsha ever spied for you?"

"I don't have spies!" he answered in an annoyed voice.

"Yeahhhhh," Marsha's supporters cheered.

"Dor-is! Dor-is!" the Doris fans began.

Again the whistle blew. "Outside! Outside!" he commanded, herding the pro-Doris group out the door. "The next person who shouts in here gets a month of detentions," he threatened to everyone who remained.

The cafeteria quieted down as kids turned their attention to the leaflets. "At least it's a fair fight now," said Rissa to Marsha.

Mike and Roger joined them. "No more fliers left," said Roger.

"Good work, guys," Rissa said, squeezing Mike's hand.

"Thanks a real lot," said Marsha.

Rissa caught sight of Bobby watching all the activity from a table at the far corner of the cafeteria. "I bet he's really proud of you now," she said to Marsha.

"No, he's not," said Marsha. "He and I are through." Marsha went on to tell Rissa and Sara about her fight with Bobby.

"That's too bad," Rissa sympathized.

Marsha shrugged. "That's the way it goes."

Later that day Rissa sat in her last period geometry class, glad that her fight with Marsha had ended. It felt much better to be friends again. Doris was in this class, but luckily the two girls sat on opposite ends of the room.

Rissa tried to listen to the teacher, but she was bored. Mr. Phipps was explaining how to do one of last night's homework problems which Rissa had done easily. She began sorting through her messy notebook, taking out the old tests and papers she no longer needed. She found some old modeling agency letters in the notebook as well. Just as she began sorting through the letters, she heard "Is that geometry you're working on?" Rissa jumped, thinking Mr. Phipps was talking to her, but when she looked up, she realized he was talking to Doris.

"Miss Gaylord? Answer me."

"Not exactly," Doris answered, blushing. She put her pencil down and placed her notebook over the piece of loose-leaf paper she'd been writing on. Rissa craned her neck to see what it was, but she couldn't see it from her seat.

"Then whatever it is, throw it into the trash," Mr. Phipps instructed her.

Wearing an annoyed expression, Doris got up, crumpled up the paper, walked to the front of the classroom, and tossed it into the trash can. "Thank you, Miss Gaylord. Now let's resume the lesson, shall we?" Mr. Phipps said. Rissa smiled, glad to see Doris in trouble.

By the end of class, Rissa had accumulated several papers that she didn't need anymore. She wadded them up, threw them into the trash can, and left the classroom, heading toward her locker. Her mind returned to the modeling letters. She'd been planning on sending out some pictures of herself to a few agencies, but lately, she'd been putting it off. She promised herself that she'd do it as soon as she found a free moment. Then, suddenly, she remembered that an address she needed was scrawled on one of the papers she'd thrown away.

Rissa turned around and rushed back to the now-empty classroom. She fished through the trash, uncrumpling several papers, looking for the sheet with the address. It didn't take long to find it, and when she reached down to take it out, something caught her eye. Rissa recognized Doris's loopy handwriting immediately. It was the sheet she'd been asked to throw away. It looked like a letter of some sort.

Rissa quickly stuck her own paper in her notebook. Then she read Doris's letter.

Dear Joey,

What's up? Haven't heard from you since our last tennis class. Is your school having elections now? Ours is. I'm running for class president. The campaign is going great. I've blown away this jerk Marsha with an ingenious tape and a well-planted rumor. Of course, it's only half true, but that's politics for you. Ha ha.

I can't wait to be president. Of course, I have to say all this stuff about wanting to serve my classmates and blah, blah, blah. But what it really means to me is that I get to vote for all the things my friends want. If my grades drop, I can blame it on being class president. And it will look great on my college application. Pretty neat, huh?

All my friends will vote for me. That's not a problem. The problem is convincing the other idiots not to vote for twerpy Marsha. I "convinced" Marty the nerd to drop out of the race, too. Most of the kids in this school are so dumb they'll believe anything you tell them, anyway. I could probably say Marsha was a foreign spy and they'd believe it. I'm sure this election

Doris hadn't had a chance to finish her letter before Mr. Phipps made her throw it away, but Rissa knew it was more than enough to incriminate Doris.

She raced to Marsha's locker and as she hoped, Marsha was there.

"Marsha!" she called, holding up the letter.

"What's that?" Marsha asked as she took the letter from Rissa. Then she began reading it.

A wicked smile crossed Marsha's face as she slipped the letter into her pocket. "Got ya, Doris," she whispered.

Chapter Nineteen

"Okay," Sara began hesitantly, addressing the band on Saturday afternoon. "Here's the campaign song I wrote. See what you think."

She stood behind the microphone in Stingo's basement and began to sing without accompaniment. "Vote for a leader. We really need her. Marsha is the one to pick, the only one who'll do the trick. Marsha is the name to trust. She leaves the others in the dust. Maaaaarsha! Oh, Maaaarsha! Vote! Now!"

Sara looked at them and immediately registered their lack of enthusiasm. "It doesn't have to be that, exactly," she said. They continued to look at her with listless expressions. "You think it drags?" she asked.

"I don't know," sighed Eric. "It's okay, I guess."

This was their first practice without Nicky and it seemed to Sara that there was a big empty space in the room. He always took charge, directed them, and kept their spirits up. Sara missed the special, encouraging smile he had for her alone.

"It needs a reggae beat," said Sam.

"I think it needs something," Stingo concurred. "I don't know what, but . . ."

Sara looked at them uneasily. They seemed to be vying to see who was the leader. What would Nicky say if he were here? She concentrated on this thought. *Come on!* he'd say. *Are we Eggheads, or what? It doesn't matter who's in charge. Let's make some music!*

Could Sara take over for him? No. She didn't think anyone could. He had a style all his own. But she had to do something. This practice was about to run out of gas before it even started.

"Here's the tune I had in mind for the song," she forced herself to continue. She hummed a few bars of a sweet catchy melody.

Again, there was silence. "You know what's wrong with it?" Stingo said after a long moment. "It's too la, la, la, blah."

Sara's first reaction was to be insulted. She decided not to let it show. An argument right now would finish this practice off in a second. "Think it can be beefed up?" she asked.

Stingo thought for a moment. "It needs more drive." He played a quick intro on the drums, ending with a crash of cymbals. "Vote for a leader!" Rumble-tum-*bang!* "We really, oh, so, so really need her!" Rap-rap-*bang!* "Marsha is the one to pick!" Smash! "She's the chick who can do the trick!" Bam! Bam! "Maaaaarsha!" Bang-bang-*bang!* "Maaarsha!" Bang-bang-*bang.* "Vote!" Bang! "Now!" *Smash!*

He looked to Sara for her reaction. "And *then* we'll do it again and pick up your second verse. How's that?"

"Much better!" Sara exclaimed sincerely. "That is much jazzier. I like what you did with the verses too. I don't think we should call her a chick, though."

"We're a rock band, we're allowed to say stuff like that," Eric disagreed.

"Hmmm," Sara thought aloud. "No, I don't like

130

it. Too insulting to women. How about 'She'll be a hit, so go for it'?''

There was more silence as they considered it. ''I can live with that,'' Stingo gave in.

''Who put you in charge?'' Eric challenged Stingo.

''What? Oh, ex*cu-use* me. I didn't realize that *you* were the leader of the band now!'' Stingo shot back sarcastically.

Sam went to his keyboard. He played a high, pulsing repetitive note. ''Something like this behind the opening?''

''Oh, now he's making the decisions,'' Stingo commented sourly.

''I like it to start, but I think it should get fuller after the first line,'' Sara suggested, ignoring Stingo's remark. She didn't want practice to degenerate into a fight. ''Stingo's right,'' she said. ''This is a rally, so we need a much bigger sound than I had originally thought. We want to get everybody all fired up.''

Sam's fingers flew over the keys. ''That's really good,'' said Sara excitedly. ''Eric, maybe it would work if you come in strong as soon as Sam opens up on the keyboard. Want to try it?''

They spent the rest of the afternoon working on the song. They changed the words and experimented with different tempos and keys. By four o'clock they were so immersed in the song that they forgot to bicker over who was in charge. They were completely in love with their new creation.

''Man, this is too good to drop after the rally,'' said Stingo. ''We can change the words just a little and keep it.'' He began to sing. ''Marsha, I need ya. Oh soooo really need ya.''

''You're the one I've waited for. You're the one that I adore,'' Sara joined in.

"Yeah." Stingo smiled. "We'll call it 'Marsha's Song.' Definitely! Let's work on it when the rally is over."

"It could be our best dance tune," said Sam.

"It's got 'single' written all over it," added Eric.

Single, Sara thought, daring to imagine the possibility of actually making a record.

"I still miss the sax, though," said Eric.

Sara sighed. "Me too. I miss him a lot."

"I guess it's the hardest for you," Stingo said consolingly.

"It's pretty lonely," Sara agreed. "Do you think we can keep on without him?"

"Hey, why not?" said Stingo. "We're not doing too bad today. You kept us going, Sara."

"Me?" said Sara, surprised but pleased.

"Hey, while us turkeys were arguing over who was the leader, you were prepared with a song. You listened to everybody's suggestions," said Sam. "You did good."

"I did, didn't I," Sara agreed, smiling. "Maybe we don't need a leader."

"Or maybe it could be you," said Stingo.

Sara left practice that evening feeling a mixed jumble of emotions. The band was going to go on. She felt confident of that now. And they'd said she'd been the one to take charge and make it work. They were right, but up until today she didn't realize she had it in her.

It occurred to her that she had Marsha to thank. If she'd been doing it strictly for herself, Sara wouldn't have found the incentive to insist that the boys go on with practice. And she certainly wouldn't have written a song. But she did it because it mattered to Marsha. Her caring about Marsha let her get something very important back. There was still going to be an Eggheads band, and she had discovered a new talent in herself. Leadership. It felt weird. But good.

She walked into her house still humming the Marsha song. "Boy, you look happy," said Elaine who was sitting at the kitchen table eating a sandwich and leafing through a clothing catalog. "I thought you were down in the dumps about Nicky."

"I am," said Sara, "but something good happened today. I guess I'm taking a break from the dumps to be happy for a while. I'll probably be in the dumps again by tonight."

"Probably," Elaine agreed, going back to her catalog. Sara had just opened the refrigerator when the phone rang. Elaine lunged to the wall phone a step ahead of Sara. "Hello," she said, and then made a face. "Yeah, she's here," she said, handing Sara the phone.

"I'm coming over," said Marsha on the other end. "Call Rissa and tell her to come too. I know exactly how we're going to win this election."

Chapter Twenty

Rissa was about to leave her house that afternoon when she encountered her father coming in the front door. "Hello, Dad," she said stiffly.

There had been a cold war going on between Rissa and her father since the day he'd demanded that she apologize. Mary had tried to smooth things over, but Rissa wanted no part of it. She avoided Mary and her father whenever possible and spoke to them in simple sentences when she had to speak at all.

"Clarissa," he acknowledged her with equal formality. He put a brown paper bag down on the hall table and continued on into the living room.

Filled with curiosity, Rissa reached into the bag and pulled out a small cream-colored box. She opened it and saw small engraved invitations. On the front of the card, in elegant calligraphy, were the words: *Mary Giffone and Peter Lupinski invite you to an informal reception at the Red Rose Restaurant at 5:00 PM, September thirtieth, to celebrate their wedding.* Inside the card was a piece of paper with directions to the restaurant.

Rissa's jaw dropped. Obviously they had decided against having a party at the house. No one had even told her about it. And September thirtieth was only two weeks away.

"Dad!" she called, heading into the kitchen. "How come you didn't tell me about the Red Rose?"

He didn't look up from the sink where he was washing his hands. "I thought you weren't coming."

"I can't believe the way you're acting!" Rissa confronted him.

"How would you like me to act, Clarissa?" he asked, staring fixedly at her with his steely blue eyes.

"I can't talk to you," cried Rissa, storming through the living room. She walked right into Roger, who was coming in the front door. "Excuse me," she said brusquely, walking past him.

"What's with you?" he asked.

"Dad. He's being a pain," she said.

"You're the one who's being a pain," he said.

Rissa stopped, surprised. Roger usually took her side in things. "I am not," she protested.

"Rissa, don't you think this is hard for him?" said Roger in a low, intense voice. "He wants Mary for a wife, but he's nervous about her fitting in here. And how do you think she feels, moving into a house with four kids? Why don't you give them a break?"

"They don't need my help," Rissa insisted. With that she whirled around and out the front door. She hurried down the street. Now Mary had turned Roger against her, too. What was his problem? Why was he turning into some kind of Mr. Goody-good all of a sudden? As she approached Sara's house, she saw Marsha coming up the block from the opposite direction.

"What's the matter?" she asked. "You look like you're fuming about something."

"I am," Rissa told her. "My father makes me so mad!" She told Marsha about their last conversation. "And Roger's on his side."

135

"Why don't you just say you're sorry," Marsha suggested.

"Because I'm not sorry. My father is the one being stubborn."

"I'd say you're both pretty stubborn," said Marsha as they headed up Sara's walkway.

"Well, nobody asked you," said Rissa.

Once they were up in Sara's bedroom, Marsha revealed her strategy. She pulled Doris's letter from the large inside pocket of her denim jacket. "I'm sure you ladies have not forgotten this super-duper secret weapon that Rissa found," she said gleefully.

"How could we." Sara laughed. "I couldn't believe my eyes when you showed it to me yesterday. It's pure Doris."

"Here's what we're going to do," said Marsha. "I'll hold onto it until the day of the rally. We'll campaign as hard as we can without using it. Then— whammo!—I read it as part of my last speech."

"Whew!" said Rissa. "You have more killer instinct than I would have thought."

"After the way Doris embarrassed me, I don't care," said Marsha. "I'm going to make sure I win this thing. When I read this, someone take a picture of her face. If this doesn't wipe her out, I don't know what will."

"That should do it," said Sara. "Who could vote for Doris after hearing that?"

"Nobody," Rissa answered.

"Exactly," said Marsha. She reached into her tote bag and pulled out a stack of large papers. "Get a load of these," she said, holding up the top sheet. In the center was an ink sketch of Marsha. "My mother gave these to me today. A friend of hers who teaches art at the college did it from a photo and my mother had them run off. I figured I needed at least something to compete with Doris's photo."

"They're great," said Sara. "Only you look like your old self, not your presidential self."

"I'm campaigning as myself," Marsha told her with conviction. "I've been thinking about it, and this trying to act like someone else is dumb. I am who I am."

"Wow! What's gotten into you?" asked Rissa.

"Nothing. I've just been doing some thinking," said Marsha. "Besides, I felt dumb talking to those kids today dressed up as a nerd."

Sara then told Marsha and Rissa about how good the Marsha song sounded. They spent the next few hours writing "Vote for Marsha" on the tops and bottoms of the sketches.

Rissa and Marsha left Sara's at six. "This is really going to work," Marsha said excitedly as they headed for home. "I can't wait for September twenty-ninth to be here."

"September twenty-ninth?" Rissa asked.

"That's the Friday of election day!" said Marsha.

"My father and Mary are getting married the next day," said Rissa.

"You'll make up with your father by then," said Marsha.

"Maybe, maybe not," Rissa replied, jamming her fists into the pockets of her jacket. They walked for a while in silence. "What are you doing tonight?" Rissa asked after a while.

"I thought I had a date," said Marsha, "but remember? I got dumped."

"Oh, yeah, sorry," said Rissa. "He didn't really dump you, though. Maybe you made him think *you* didn't want to go."

"Fat chance," said Marsha. "And I liked him so much too. He didn't know me well enough to know what to believe when that sign went up, I guess."

"Think he'll come around when he sees our signs?" Rissa asked.

Marsha shrugged. "Even if he did, I wouldn't feel the same. And no matter what the signs say, he thinks the whole election is stupid—remember? He bailed out when things got rough, so who cares about him."

"That's right," Rissa agreed, but from the sadness in Marsha's eyes, she could see that her friend didn't mean it. She put her hand on her shoulder. "Falling in love stinks sometimes," she said sympathetically.

"I'll say," Marsha agreed. They had reached the corner where they'd go their separate ways.

"Talk to you tomorrow," said Rissa, waving. She quickened her pace as she headed down the street toward home. She was supposed to be ready to go out with Mike at six-thirty. They had a date to go to the Rosemont Twin.

When she got home she heard the sound of the TV coming from the back den. Her brother Roger was watching a football game. "Hi," she said, plopping down on the old couch beside him.

He grunted a hello, his eyes remaining glued to the set. Still staring at the screen, he handed her a long white envelope. "This was stuck in my copy of *Sports Illustrated* by mistake," he explained absently.

Rissa looked at the envelope. "The Mellors Agency" and an address was printed in the upper left-hand corner. The name sounded vaguely familiar to her. She tore open the envelope and pulled out a piece of light yellow stationery with an address and phone number on top. She began to read the letter.

Dear Ms. Sky:

In our search for fresh, teen talent, we came across your picture in an ad for *Teen Today*. We contacted *Teen Today*, and they have no objection to your signing with our agency. We believe you have the potential to become a successful model. We look forward to hearing from you and hope you will agree to come aboard as a Mellors Model. Please contact us at the number above.

A Mellors Model! That's where she'd heard the term! She'd read about the Mellors Agency in a magazine article about super-models. They were one of the biggest and best agencies in New York.

"Roger!" Rissa cried, jumping to her feet. "The Mellors Agency wants me! I'm going to be a Mellors Model."

"Great," said Roger blandly.

"You could be a little excited for me," Rissa said angrily.

"Look! I said it was great, okay?" said Roger, using the remote control to switch to a game on another station.

His attitude annoyed Rissa. "What good is it having great things happen to you when the people around you can't even be happy for you?"

Roger looked her square in the eyes. "I don't know," he said pointedly. "Why don't you ask Dad that question."

Chapter Twenty-One

Marsha spent the next week campaigning hard. But so did Doris. Any blank wall space that didn't feature Doris's photo poster had a poster with the sketch of Marsha's face. Although Doris's posters were more professional-looking, Marsha hoped her poster was at least unusual enough to be memorable.

Marsha stayed late after school almost every day addressing the various clubs. She had to be careful not to bump into Doris who was also talking to the clubs. Marsha was surprised at how many issues there really were to discuss. The Girls' Sports Club wanted an allotment of the student activity fund for new gymnastic equipment. The Drama Club felt the students, not the teachers, should pick the productions. The Photography Society wanted to use the darkroom during lunch and study periods. The issues went on and on. Marsha kept a list and promised to bring every issue up before the student council.

Marsha wasn't sure when it happened, but somewhere along the line a change occurred in her. She stopped worrying about her image and became concerned about the issues. She was so busy talking to students and finding out what they wanted, that it took up all her time and energy.

Doris tried to revive the old "Marsha the Snitch"

campaign for a while, but it didn't take. A number of kids came up to Marsha and said they would have done the same thing in her shoes. Sue Harmon ran a story on the campaign in the *Rosemont Reporter*. It generated a series of letters to the editor on the "snitching" incident. Those students who agreed with Marsha and those who didn't were almost evenly divided. Marsha was pleased to see that no one referred to her as Mr. Ames's private spy. And apparently the tape had worked against Doris. A number of students wrote in calling it a sleazy tactic.

Marsha's feelings still took a bruising once in a while. One day she tore down a poster on which someone had added a mustache and beard to her picture. And Doris put up a poster saying: WANT TO BE THE LAUGHING STOCK OF THE SCHOOL? THEN VOTE FOR KRANTON AS SOPHOMORE PREZ.

When Marsha saw that sign, she patted her purse which contained Doris's letter. It was her secret weapon to be revealed at exactly the right moment.

Bobby Turner missed biology the week after their canceled date. Whenever she saw him in the hall she looked away, never making eye contact. But that didn't stop her from thinking about him. One night she dreamed that they were riding down the street on his motorcycle, the wind whipping her hair. She daydreamed about him in class too. She tried to turn her feelings off, but she just couldn't do it.

On the Thursday before the election, she arrived to science lab a few minutes early. She stuck her head into the class, hoping he wasn't there.

No luck. He sat at the empty table, his legs sprawled into the aisle, looking dreamily out the window. "Oh, hi," he said when she sat down quietly beside him.

"Hi," she said, melting just a little from the sad look in those dreamy eyes, despite her efforts not to.

"Even though I haven't seen you, I see you everywhere," he said. "Every time I turn around, there's your picture."

"I guess you must be sick of me by now." Marsha laughed uneasily.

"No, I like seeing you," he said. He turned in his chair so that he was looking right at her. "Look, Marsha, just because you don't want to go out with me anymore, doesn't mean we can't be friends. I was mad at first when you dumped me, but what the heck, I mean—"

"Whoa!" said Marsha. "Slow down. You dumped me, remember?"

His eyes narrowed in confusion. "No. You were the one who said we didn't have much in common."

"I only said that to let you off the hook," she admitted. "I knew you were embarrassed to be seen with me after the whole school said I was a stool pigeon."

"That stupid thing?" He laughed. "You forget that I'm a junior," he said with a hint of pride. "We don't pay all that much attention to what you little sophomores do."

"Excuse me?" said Marsha, pretending to be insulted.

"Except that I care what one little sophomore does. Because I like her," he said, shyly.

"*Little* sophomore!" cried Marsha, with a smile in her eyes. "But you still think I'm dumb for running in this campaign, don't you?"

"I get a little carried away with my opinions sometimes," he said. "And I hated to see Doris put you through so much aggravation. I'm sorry."

Marsha felt her smile spread from ear to ear. "I'm sorry too," she said.

He took her hand and squeezed it under the lab table as the class filled with students. "Will you come to my rally tomorrow?" she asked.

"Absolutely," he answered. "I think it's great they gave us a half day to hold these elections. Hey, if you become president, can I be the first man of the sophomore class?"

"If you want to be!" Marsha laughed.

That night, Sara and Rissa came over to Marsha's house. "Let's make sure we're all set," said Rissa, going over a list she had on a long yellow pad. "The band is going to be set up in the parking lot by noon."

"Check," said Sara.

"And Marsha can use your microphone for her speech?"

"Yep," Sara confirmed. "Do you know what you're going to say, Marsha?"

Marsha nodded.

"Then I'd say we're all set," Rissa said, heading for the door.

"What time is it?" asked Sara, panicked.

"Seven," said Marsha.

"I have to get home," cried Sara, grabbing her jacket and running for the door. "Nicky wrote and said he might be able to call me at nine from his father's office."

"Sara, that's two hours from now," Rissa pointed out.

"I know, but I want to give myself, you know, a lot of space in case he's early or something." She ran past Rissa and bolted down the stairs. "See you tomorrow," she called from the hallway.

Marsha laughed. "That's Sara for you."

"Yeah," Rissa agreed with a weak smile.

"You still haven't settled this wedding mess, have you?" Marsha said, guessing the problem.

"I heard Mary telling my father to drop it, but he's such a stubborn mule. She was crying and everything. They didn't know I was in the hallway listening. The wedding is only two days away."

"You have to go," said Marsha. "This is crazy."

"It's not my fault," Rissa insisted. "He started it."

"I don't know." Marsha sighed. "It sounds like such a mess."

"I didn't make the mess, though," said Rissa. "It's up to him to tell me he wants me at that wedding."

"You and your father are like clones. You're what Pete Lupinski would be like if he were trapped in the body of a fourteen-year-old girl."

"I'm forgetting you said that," said Rissa. "I know you're just nervous about tomorrow."

"Maybe so," said Marsha. "I'll see you tomorrow." As soon as Rissa left, Marsha got ready for bed. She hoped to get a good night's sleep to prepare her for tomorrow.

Chapter Twenty-Two

Marsha tossed and turned all night, but by morning she was bursting with energy. She was happy to see it was a clear, crisp autumn morning. She dressed quickly, wearing the fitted dusty-blue corduroy dress with the snaps up the front which she'd bought the week before. Her parents wished her luck as she dashed past them after gulping down a glass of orange juice. They had both wanted to come, but Marsha said it might make her nervous.

Her morning classes went by in a blur. At twelve, Marsha walked out the back door and past the different rally spots which were spread out across the soccer field. At each rally spot there was a table and a few chairs. Students were busy hanging banners, finishing signs, and milling about from one candidate headquarters to another. Marsha spotted Sara setting up equipment with the other Eggheads. "Nicky called!" Sara said excitedly as Marsha approached her.

"Great!" said Marsha. "How is he?"

"Okay. He's homesick, but he says it's exciting," Sara answered. "He's going to call me once a week. His father said he could."

"See. It won't be so bad," Marsha said, glad to see real happiness in Sara's eyes for the first time since Nicky left. Marsha peered over at Doris's campaign headquarters. "I wonder what she's going to do for this event," she said to Sara.

"I heard a rumor that Doris had her own video made," Sara said.

"It must be true," said Rissa, approaching them, with Mike at her side. "They're putting up the screen now." A wide white screen was being set up near Doris's area.

"Don't worry, we'll blow them away," Stingo assured Marsha.

A few minutes later, the different rallies began. Each candidate had been allotted his or her own time slot. First the two freshman candidates made their speeches. A squad of freshmen cheerleaders did a routine for one of them. The other belonged to the chorus, and had a group come out to sing Rosemont's school song.

Then a large crowd gathered around Doris. She played her video, which featured Doris going through a school day. She smiled at the students, waved, talked earnestly to teachers, and looked sincere to the accompaniment of popular songs.

"I think I'm going to be sick," Sara said to Stingo.

Doris had a hand-held microphone as she addressed her group. "I want you to know," she said in her sweetest voice, "that I'm going to work my darndest to make sophomores the most outstanding class in this school. I truly care about each and every one of you. I'm not only for the brains and the teachers' pets like my opponent is. I represent the average student. The normal kids—just like me. Thank you." Doris's followers cheered wildly.

"So now I'm not normal," Marsha muttered through clenched teeth. "That girl has nerve."

Finally, it was Marsha's turn and the Eggheads began to play. A crowd from all the grades gathered around them almost immediately. "Marsha's Song" was a big hit, attracting a large and enthusiastic audience.

When they were done, Marsha stepped up to the microphone. "This campaign has been a great learning experience for me," she began. "I've learned a great deal about myself in the course of this campaign. I've discovered that I'm a lot stronger than I ever imagined."

I've also learned a few startling things about Doris Gaylord when I accidently came across a letter written by my opponent. Let me read it to you.

That was what she had intended to say at that point. But suddenly it seemed all wrong. She had something more important to say and she didn't have a lot of time to say it.

"I've also learned about people and how they can either work together or fumble around alone, wrestling with problems all by themselves. That's what student government is all about. It's about listening to each other—talking things out, finding ways to solve problems together. We all have our own concerns and our own points of view. As class president, I promise to try to step out of my own viewpoint and really listen—really try to see problems from the other person's point of view. That's not always easy to do, but I promise to try."

The crowd applauded and cheered. The Eggheads sang the last lines of the Marsha song again. Rissa came up to Marsha. "You couldn't use the secret weapon, huh," she asked.

"I didn't want to act like Doris," Marsha said. "I just couldn't do it."

"I knew you wouldn't," said Rissa.

"You did? How?" Marsha asked.

"Because I know you," Rissa answered.

Marsha saw Bobby waving to her. She ran over to greet him. "Great speech." He smiled.

"I hope it was great enough," she said. "They're starting to vote now. We should know by three."

At the inside back door, students could get ballots which they dropped into a large box. A staff of volunteers began counting them immediately. Marsha walked in, picked up a sheet, and circled her own name. "Smile!" said a boy from the *Rosemont Reporter* as he snapped her picture.

Nervously she handed in her ballot and went back to her rally site to await the results.

At three o'clock, Mr. Shepherd, the student council coordinator, came out of the school. He walked to a microphone that had been set up by the door. "The votes have been tabulated," he began.

Marsha felt her hands shake. She was standing alongside Sara and Rissa. She grabbed their hands nervously.

First he read the freshman winner. Marsha barely heard it.

"And the new sophomore class president is . . . Marsha Kranton!" he announced.

At first his words didn't sink in. Marsha heard him, but it didn't seem real. But the next thing she knew Rissa was hugging her and screaming joyfully into her ear. "You won! You won! You won!"

A slow smile spread across her face. She had beaten Doris. She had done it—plain old Marsha Kranton had beaten glamorous, popular Doris. It was true. It was really happening. And she'd done it fairly.

She realized Bobby had come up beside her. Marsha's eyes met his. "Congratulations," he said warmly.

"Thanks," she said, beaming a smile at him. "It *is* more than a personality contest, you know."

"Maybe you're right." He smiled.

Sara dragged Marsha to the microphone as the students cheered. "I'll work real hard," she shouted. "Thank you. Thanks a lot!"

The Eggheads repeated the Marsha song while her friends applauded. Marsha was hugged and congratulated by a flood of people.

Her head was spinning, and she felt as if she were dreaming. But she knew she wasn't. Somehow she knew this was a turning point in her life. She was still the person she'd always been, but she was on her way to being her best self. She felt it in her bones, and it felt good.

Marsha knew she owed so much to Rissa and Sara. They'd been with her through this, and together they'd jumped the hurdles. This experience had taught her a lot about them as well as about herself.

She saw Sara leading a cheer of "Marsha! Marsha!" over at the microphone. Then Marsha looked around for Rissa—but she was gone.

Chapter Twenty-Three

Rissa hurried home from school. She was thrilled for Marsha, but now she had an important task and it couldn't wait. "Dad," she called, coming in the front door. She knew he'd taken the day off. She hoped he was home.

"We're in here," Mary called from the dining room. Rissa found them sitting at the table going over the guest list.

"Can I talk to you, Dad?" she asked.

"I have to call the restaurant," Mary excused herself tactfully.

Her father walked to the living room and seated himself on the couch. "Dad, I'm sorry I've been so mean," she began.

"Don't tell me, tell Mary," he said sternly.

"I'll tell Mary in a minute," she said. "Why do you have to make this so hard?"

"Because you've hurt me, Clarissa," he answered. "You are trying to spoil a very happy time for me."

Rissa was silent a moment. "I'm sorry," she said. "I really am." She felt her lip start to quiver, but she was determined not to cry. "I just don't want to be forced to be someone I'm not. I was trying to make that clear."

"Did you have to be so rude about it?" he asked.

Rissa looked away. "No. I suppose I was upset because . . . because . . ." Rissa's voice caught in her throat.

"Because why?" her father asked.

"Because I don't want you to forget about me," she said in a choked voice.

Her father stood and faced the window. "We're two of a kind, aren't we?" he said finally. "It didn't really occur to me how bad you must have been feeling too." He went to her and wrapped his arms around her. "You'll always be my one and only Clarissa Jean," he said soothingly. A gentle laugh escaped his lips.

"I guess we are alike," Rissa said, wiping her eyes. "I feel so awful about the way I treated Mary. I'll go apologize right now."

Mr. Lupinski smiled. "I'm sure she'll understand."

She went to the kitchen and found Mary staring out the window unhappily.

"Mary, I'm sorry I was so mean to you," she said. "I know my father loves you very much. I promise I won't make your life miserable."

"I just don't think sometimes," said Mary. "I forget that everyone doesn't like the same things I do. I'll try to remember that, Rissa."

"Me too," said Rissa.

"Then maybe we'll get to really know each other," Mary said. She extended her hand to shake. Rissa took it. "Welcome to the family," Rissa said sincerely.

That night Rissa called Marsha. "Sorry I left so early," she said, "but I made up with my father and Mary."

"I'm glad," said Marsha happily. "The only thing you missed was the look on Doris's face when I handed her the letter. I thought she was going to keel over."

"I wish I had seen it," Rissa squealed. "I can't believe you did that!"

"Hey," laughed Marsha. "I'm a president, not a saint."

"You're invited to the reception tomorrow," she told Marsha. "Call Sara and ask her to come too. Sorry it's so last-minute but I didn't know if I was going. You can come to the ceremony in the chapel too, but I think you'd be bored. It won't be fun until the food comes out."

The next morning the Lupinski house was even more chaotic than usual. Mr. Lupinski was as pale as a ghost and seemed to wander back and forth through the hall looking for one thing or another.

Rissa helped the boys by telling them what to wear. "You don't like anything I put on!" Ralph complained.

"I'm sorry, but you cannot wear jeans to this wedding," Rissa insisted, rummaging through his drawer for clean pants.

Finally everyone piled into the family's old blue station wagon and headed for the chapel. Mary was already there. She looked pretty in a blue chiffon dress with ruffles down the front. A smattering of friends and relatives were sprinkled throughout the pews.

Rissa sat next to her brothers in the front row as her father and Mary stood in front of the small, simple altar. The ceremony was about to begin when Sara and Marsha slid into the pew behind Rissa.

"Hey, you guys," she greeted them softly.

"Is it okay if we're here?" Sara whispered.

"Sure," said Rissa. "I just thought it would be boring for you."

"We thought you might need your friends," said Marsha.

Rissa smiled at them. "I do. Thanks."

"You don't have to thank us," said Marsha.

"We're friends, aren't we?" Sara said.

"The best friends," Rissa agreed. "The best friends in the whole world."

SUZANNE WEYN has written several books for children and young adults, including *The Makeover Club* and *The Makeover Summer,* the Avon Flare prequels to *The Makeover Campaign.* She also teaches a class on "Writing for Young People" at New York University. Suzanne lives in Putnam Valley with her husband, William Gonzalez, and their daughter Diana.